Paul Mannering was born, as we so often are, to biological parents (literally, his father was a Marine Biologist).

The youngest of 4 surviving children and an unknown number of others who never made it past zygote, or were simply sold for research purposes to make ends meet. (The 70's were a hard time for his family). Born in Kaikoura, New Zealand, where steep mountains plunge into dark seas with canyons so deep that colossal squid and whales duel it out in the crushing depths.

Moving to Christchurch at 14, after a year of boarding school, he fought his way through high-school and then started the first of many full time jobs. He became a father at 19, went through various life experiences, went to a community college as an adult student, studied nursing, traveled overseas, returned, worked and did all the fun things that you do when you are in your 20's and 30's.

Realising that he really missed writing, Paul started taking it seriously again in his late 30's. Since then he has had a dozen novels published, a pile of short stories released into the wild, and he has written and produced a lot of podcast audio drama. He even won awards.

Paul has recently relocated to Australia from New Zealand where he now lives under an assumed identity as a functional adult in Canberra, Australian Capital Territory.

THE DRAKEFORTH SERIES
PUBLISHED BY IFWG

Engines of Empathy (Book 1)
Pisce of Fate (Book 2)
Time of Breath (Book 3)

THE DRAKEFORTH SERIES BOOK 3

TIME OF BREATH

BY PAUL MANNERING

Time of Breath

All Rights Reserved

ISBN-13: 978-1-925956-39-9

Copyright ©2019 Paul Mannering

V1.0

Printed in Palatino Linotype and Voodoo Eye Title

IFWG Publishing International
Melbourne
www.ifwgpublishing.com

ACKNOWLEDGEMENTS

Thanks to everyone who made this book possible. Gerry Huntman of IFWG for taking on the series after two books. Noel the Editor, for diligent Google-Fu.

For the world at large for giving me enough material to fill a library of books about the curious nature of the Universe. And to the readers, particularly the ones I have never met, who were under no obligation to buy the book, but did anyway.

Of course, if you got your copy through a book pirating site, may you have a long and utterly tedious existence with absolutely nothing but regret and adult diapers at the end of it.

For Bill Hollweg
Artist and dreamer.

CHAPTER 1

In many cultures, Death is represented by a human figure who carries gardening tools, though the exact implement differs between each culture and country. If Death carries a pruning saw in Escrustia, a rake in Nytolix or a watering can according to the mythology of Phooget, each is equally symbolic of Death's role as the harvester of souls.

The truth, of course, is that death cannot exist without life, and life exists best when all the factors are balanced. Nothing balances the factors like aerated soil, well-pruned branches, and a sprinkle of fresh water.

Like any dedicated horticulturist, Death comes for us all and generally cannot be avoided. Metaphorically, it is the same as spotting an ex-paramour across the room at a party, leaving you lurking by the kitchen for the rest of the evening while they have a great time dancing in front of the stereo all night with the one person who seems remotely interesting.

I sipped my drink and peered around the kitchen door into the darkened living room. My escape route was blocked by people who enjoyed nothing more than having a few drinks with old friends, while making new ones by dancing with them.

The only thing that could possibly make my evening more intolerable, was currently dancing with an interesting woman in front of the stereo.

"I'm guessing," a man said in my ear while he weaved drunkenly half a beat behind the music.

"What?" I said, without breaking my surveillance of the living room.

"I'm Lyal Guessing. This is my friend's party."

"Oh, that's nice." I moved closer to the kitchen door, calculating the quickest way out of the apartment.

"I'm guessing you're in need of a drink." Lyal gave a thin laugh. He let it taper out through his nose, giving me plenty of time to join in. If I wanted. Anytime now…

"Gus, could you do me a favour?"

"Lyal," he corrected.

"Lyal," I agreed. "Could you do me a favour?"

Lyal nodded with the deliberate focus of the happily drunk.

"Go away."

"Right. Yes…okay." Lyal nodded and turned to his left.

Finding his way blocked by a couple making out, he twisted right and blinked at the fridge. The awkwardness of his entrapment elicited another sinus-flute chuckle.

"Gestating gerbils," I muttered as the dancing couple paused for breath and he gestured towards the kitchen, where there were drinks to be had.

For me, the kitchen was the washed-out bridge on the only road out of town. I had nowhere to go and no way to avoid him.

Taking a deep breath, I moved closer to Lyal.

"Kiss me," I said, glancing over my shoulder towards the door.

"What?" Lyal blinked.

"Kiss me, please. Now."

Lyal's nostrils flared in readiness for a guffaw. I stifled it by pressing my lips against his.

"Charlotte?" The couple had reached the kitchen, and it was the young man with the sweptback hair who had spoken.

I twisted away from Lyal's enthusiastic mouth. "Oh, hey, Kip."

"How…are you?" Kip asked. The young woman with him gave a polite smile that barely reached her lips.

"I'm…great." A smile stretched towards my ears like the straps on a surgical mask.

"I didn't know you were going to be here," Kip said.

"Neither did I, but you know me: if there's a party, I'll be there," I replied. My enthusiasm as fake as an astro-turf toupee.

"Okay…" Kip looked around for something suitable to keep the conversation afloat. "Oh, this is uhm… This is my friend." Kip presented the dark-haired woman with as much of a flourish as the close quarters of the kitchen would allow.

"Hi," I smiled. The woman simply nodded. "This is Lyal…?"

"Hey." Lyal leaned past me and shook Kip's hand vigorously. The woman folded her arms before he could even try to take hers.

"Great party," Kip said.

"Yeah," I agreed. My relationship with Kip Alehouse had been brief and awkward. We were both taking papers in Dialectics, the science of verbal communication styles, and I broke up with Kip the same morning I decided to change my major to Computer Psychology.

"It's nice to see you again, Charl'," Kip said.

I winced. Of all the ways my name could be verbally amputated, leave it to Kip to find the one that set my teeth on edge.

"You too." I gave him the thumbs up and squirmed out of Lyal's embrace.

I looked past Kip in the vain hope I could see a reason to excuse myself and leave. It took a moment, and then I noticed that the dark-haired woman standing with Kip was also standing with the other people at party-central around the living room.

I blinked and stared harder: it wasn't just a group of dark-haired, pale-skinned women wearing black, though the college had enough of those for cloning to be a plausible explanation.

"That's weird," I said. No one commented and I returned my attention to Kip. The dark-haired woman leaned in and whispered something in his ear. My jaw dropped as Kip faded in a swirl of multi-coloured sparks, and a moment later, his clothes stood empty as if his outfit had been put on an invisible mannequin.

I waved a hand; it shed skin cells in a rainbow of sparks. "I think someone spiked my drink."

Lyal Guessing had also vanished, his rumpled suit continuing to grind incoherently without him.

I struggled to breathe against a tightening band around my chest. A desperate moment later, my focus cleared as, wide-eyed and choking, I tried to speak. The pale woman smiled at me, reached out and—

CHAPTER 2

*H*issss.
Clank.
Gurrrble.
Whup-feee-ooooh. WUNG!
Click.

Light: cold, clinical, and serious. This light did not care for mixing with colours. This light had a job to do and took pride in doing it well.

I closed my eyes tighter against the unwelcome intrusion. The air following the light into my space was colder than the antiseptic glow.

"Mughpf?" I asked through the mask covering my mouth and nose.

A silhouette blocked the light. Even through clenched eyelids, I could sense the figure was leaning over me. Hands removed the mask, and a tube attached to it exhaled the sweet scent of mint with a sigh.

The hands came back; this time they lifted me out of the warm gel-bath I had floated in, as secure and contained as a foetus. With a firm grip, the silhouette set me on my feet. I barely felt my numb legs give way immediately.

Sitting on the floor, I waited for my brain to process the latest updates. The floor, my skin reported, was cold and made of some kind of tile. *Oh, and you are naked.*

I opened my eyes in preparation of being horrified. Everything was a blur, as it took a moment for my brain to kick-start the eyes.

The silhouette leaned down as the light made an effort to be accommodating. The pale woman from the party looked into my eyes. I blinked, the woman didn't. I had time to notice that the woman's irises were dark to the point of being black. Her pupils had the shape of silvery human skulls.

She lifted me smoothly to my feet and handed me a towel. She stood silently while I cleaned the worst of the pink goo off myself.

"Contacts," I said. "You're wearing contacts."

The woman gave a slight smile and took the towel away. She offered a white robe of the fluffy kind that I had never seen outside of a sensie starring one of those impossibly perfect-bodied people who, I secretly hoped, were computer enhanced, if not generated.

Wearing the robe made me feel warm and luxurious to the knees.

"Did you ever have one of those experiences, where you wake up and everything seems distinctly...odd?" I waved a hand. "Like, when you fall asleep in the afternoon, and wake up and it's still kind of light. Then you think it might be morning and you get up to go to class and about the point you're trying to decide between breakfast cereal, or just tea..." I trailed off as the spots dancing in front of my eyes reminded me to inhale.

The woman took my hand and led me across the floor. Contact with the cold tiles prodded me into thinking more clearly.

"Arthur's toes... I'm dead?"

The woman holding my hand turned back and smiled in a complex expression. Enigmatic, not quite friendly, more amused and accommodating, without slipping into condescension.

It was a great look and I wondered how she did it.

We reached the shower without further comment or facial calisthenics. The woman left me to wash and rinse.

Ten minutes later, I emerged fresh and towelled dry. As I dressed in the clothes I found on a hook outside the shower, I thought about which of the many questions deserved to be asked first.

Stepping out, I went with an easy one: "Who are you?"

The woman was regarding a painting on the wall, a mass-produced print of Lego Gonious' famous painting of a bear play-ing some kind of harp while a woman swings upside down from the limb of a living oak tree with her hands holding her white dress modestly around the crux of her pale thighs.

It was the kind of image that I thought would make an effective poster for a campaign warning kids to avoid recreational drugs.

I clicked a mental stopwatch; sufficient time for a polite response had passed.

"I only ask, because I'm sure it's going to be important. When I tell this story to people later. At work during lunch, or at parties... Wait, we met at a party...?"

The woman turned around and walked to the door. Opening it, she indicated that I should step through. With one last look at the empathic energy extraction tank that I had recently been in, I followed her out.

Part of me wondered if some kind of afterlife was awaiting us on the other side of the door. However, if the salmon-green colour on the walls and the inexcusable carpet pattern were any indication, what came after death wasn't as much fun as people hoped.

The silent woman retrieved a pair of flight tickets from her coat. She handed them to me, and then deftly took one back.

"We're going somewhere?" I asked. "Of course we are going somewhere. I mean *where* are we going?" I shook my head in self-irritation, and then opened the packet with the ticket in it. "Pathia? Why in the herbalist are we going to Pathia?"

The woman extended an arm and pointed, unwaveringly, in a South-westerly direction.

"I said why, not where. Besides, I don't have anything packed. I mean, I wasn't expecting to come back from my last trip."

The arm moved with a compass-needle sweep to point north-northwest, and then angled downwards. I followed the hand and saw a set of cacolet-leather luggage waiting on the floor.

"Well, okay." I took a moment to consider why none of this seemed at all odd. "No, it's not that it doesn't seem odd. It's just I have built up some kind of tolerance to odd."

The woman walked to another door, which proved to be an exit. I picked up the luggage and followed her into the street.

CHAPTER 3

A growing crowd of angry people gesticulating at a parked taxi told me all I needed to know about where Vole Drakeforth might be.

"So sorry, excuse me." I apologised, pushing my way through to the eye of the storm.

Drakeforth screwed a monocle deeper into his eye socket and wriggled the fake moustache he was wearring under a leather chauffeur's cap. "I can explain it to you, but I can't understand it for you," he declared.

"You cut me off!" an angry driver shouted.

"Where did you get your licence?" another demanded.

"Scared me half to death!" a woman holding a bicycle added.

Drakeforth waved their concerns away like buzzing flies.

"Once again. It is true that I am driving, in the sense that I am travelling through a multi-dimensional spatial patrix that, even if you could perceive the full scope of it, you could not possibly hope to understand." This casual dismissal of their concerns drove the crowd into a howling frenzy.

I forged through, passing Drakeforth and going to the rear of the vehicle, which was jutting out into the street and clogging the flow of traffic like a tennis ball in a downpipe.

After opening the trunk and transferring my luggage inside, I got into the back seat and waited for Drakeforth to finish being annoying.

The angry voices increased in volume while Drakeforth turned his back on the crowd.

"Thank you, thank you," he waved and smiled. He opened the door and got behind the wheel.

"Hello, Drakeforth," I said.

"Pudding," he replied, and started the engine. Without referencing the rear-vision mirrors, the car lurched backwards. The air filled with the polite coughing of various car horns and the hysterical shriek of emergency braking.

Slipping the gear stick into drive, Drakeforth hit the accelerator and the cab leapt forward as it if had been stung.

"Wait!" I yelped. "The woman from the party…" I blinked; my silent companion was sitting next to me and regarding the blurred vista with interest.

"Do you have your ticket?" Drakeforth asked.

"The zippelin ticket to Pathia? Yes, but why?"

Drakeforth's response was lost in the squealing of tyres as we hurtled around a corner and drove the wrong way up a one-way street.

"Wrong way!" I cried.

"That is entirely a matter of perspective," Drakeforth replied calmly.

"Well, from the perspective of the oncoming traffic, we are going the wrong way."

"You left me a letter." Drakeforth put the kind of accusation into that simple statement that I usually only heard when addressing myself.

I started with, "Well, yes?"

"A letter, Pudding. After everything we went through, you thought a simple narrative about our adventures, followed by a brief explanation of where you had gone, was somehow going to make up for the deceit of it all?"

"That was the plan." In fact, I thought the plan had been quite good. By the time Drakeforth finished reading my record, I would be well gone into the empathic matrix of the Python building and would be well out of it.

The hum of the engine rose to a higher pitch and the car charged faster at the oncoming traffic in a re-enactment of those nature documentaries where a predator breaks cover in the climactic moment.

"We are going to die," I whispered. The pale woman passenger turned her head and raised an eyebrow.

The taxi bounced over the curb, sliding sideways from one streetlight pole to the next. Startled noises rained down in a way the survivors of the Cat Storm of Kabutz remember all too well[1].

Drakeforth twisted the wheel, sending the taxi back into the street. We careened through a narrow gap between a dairy van and a truck carrying a load of ice. I screamed and had a sudden flashback to summer holidays in the back yard with Mum, Dad, and Ascott.

The taxi roared into the next intersection before, like a duck taking flight, it settled into a smooth path in line with other traffic.

After a few seconds to unclench, I started to breathe again. The interior of the taxi flickered with a green strobe light. Twisting in my seat, I stared out the rear window at a fast approaching police car.

"Drakeforth, I think they want you to stop."

"Stop what?" he replied, swerving through the lanes of traffic.

"Being you?" I suggested.

"Ha!" Drakeforth barked. The traffic lights ahead of us changed and the traffic dutifully slowed to a halt. Drakeforth leaned on the horn and the car cleared its throat.

I watched as two officers, a man and a woman, exited the vehicle behind us and approached the taxi, one on each side.

"If anyone asks, you haven't seen me," Drakeforth announced.

"Sure." An hour ago, I had been in what the Godden corporation technicians described as a state of transition. Now all I wanted was a cup of tea and a nap.

---

1 In 936, according to the calendar of Nyk, Johann Kabutz (hailed as a brilliant scientist or a raving moon-bug, depending on who you ask) sought to determine the exact factors that would best define "raining cats and dogs". While his results were inconclusive, the safety gear he developed for the animals he launched en-masse into the sky led him to invent the parachute.

The male officer rapped on the driver's window. Drakeforth lowered it and peered up at the green uniform, with its line of shiny brass buttons.

"Good morning, sir," the officer intoned.

"Is it? I hadn't noticed," Drakeforth replied with a tone of mild surprise.

"Indeed…" the officer took his time unclipping a leather holster on his belt and extracting a notebook and a pen. He then clicked the pen before carefully lifting the cover on the notebook, as if wary of what might leap out at him.

"Well, goodbye then," Drakeforth said, and closed the window. The traffic continued to wait in an orderly queue for the changing of the lights.

I squinted through the window on the other side; the female officer peered back at me through the glass. I felt a sudden affinity with a museum exhibit.

The first officer tapped on the driver's window again. Drakeforth did a double take and opened the window.

"I have the strangest sense of didgeridoo."

"Do you know why we stopped your vehicle, sir?" the officer asked, pen poised to take notes.

"You didn't. The lights changed. We stopped."

"I see, sir. Not quite the reason, sir. Do you know exactly how fast you were going?"

"At which point?" Drakeforth replied. "*Exactly*?" he added after a moment for emphasis.

The police officer rumbled and refocused his attention on the spot where the pen waited to write on the notebook page.

"The suspect vehicle was witnessed travelling the wrong way down Perversas Street. During the duration of the traverse, the vehicle diverted from the traffic lane and entered the pedestrian zone of the sidewalk. Further to—"

"You spelt *pedestrian* wrong," Drakeforth said, interrupting the officer's dictation and note-taking.

"What?" The officer stopped writing and frowned.

"*P-E-D-E-S-T-R-A-I-N*," Drakeforth spelled out.

"Pedes-train?" The officer frowned at the page.

"Yes, from the Ancient Gherkin. *Pedes*, meaning *to clump together*, and *train*, meaning *to annoy the caviar out of everyone else trying to use the sidewalk*."

"I...believe the spelling, *P-E-D-E-S-T-R-I-A-N*, *pedestrian*, is correct, sir."

"Officer, a spelling error in their notes would be acceptable for most people. But for someone who clearly takes as much pride in all aspects of their work as you do, such a black mark is unforgivable."

The officer stared at the page of notes and then returned his concerned gaze to Drakeforth, who remained suitably solemn.

With a deliberate neatness, the policeman eased the offending page from the notebook's wire binding and crumpled it in one hand.

"Perhaps I can take that for you?" Drakeforth offered. "We don't want to have you write yourself up on a littering charge, now, do we?"

"Uh, no. Thank you sir," the policeman said, offering the crumpled piece of paper.

"Now, what was it you wanted to ask me?" Drakeforth asked.

The lights changed and the traffic moved forward. Drakeforth drove off, his head still inclined towards the officer in green.

I settled back in my seat with a sigh. "You should probably take the next exit, less chance of being followed if you cut through the avocado district."

"They won't follow us," Drakeforth replied. "That clipper is still trying to work out what just happened. He's got the sort of pride that will refuse to accept humiliation."

I covered a yawn with my hand. "I hope so, we don't want to miss our flight." Closing my eyes was all the encouragement sleep needed. I had a vague sensation of falling as I tilted sideways until my head rested on the silent woman's shoulder. She firmly pushed me back onto an even keel and I found a comfortable spot with my head pressed against the window.

CHAPTER 4

"Airports," Drakeforth declared with his hands on his hips.

I finished extracting my luggage from the trunk of the taxi while Drakeforth stood looking around.

"I haven't been on a zippelin since before Mum and Dad passed."

"And whose fault is that?" Drakeforth asked.

I started explaining in detail how having a job, a mortgage, and all the myriad things that make life the grinding chore it is, left little time for zipping off to exotic locations on a whim. Drakeforth was already vanishing through the automatic doors that led into the terminal. My silent companion appeared to be listening, though, so I felt less stupid than usual.

Loading the bags onto a trolley reminded me of why nobody enjoyed their time at airports. The cacolet-leather set had a large suitcase, two smaller suitcases and a carry on bag with little wheels and an extendable handle. Perfect for someone with four arms and a centre of gravity located around their ankles.

The courtesy luggage trolley provided by airports is one of the great ironies of life. By definition, a courtesy is an act of kindness towards others. By example, an airport luggage trolley is an act of malicious rudeness bordering on aggravated assault.

I placed the first of the suitcases on the trolley and then squeezed the smaller two in front of it. Reaching for the fourth meant the third fell off. Setting the fourth down, and repacking the third, I discovered that for some reason it now didn't fit.

I precariously balanced the fourth case in the basket near the bar handle and laid the second case flat. Placing the third on top of it, I eyed the set-up warily. Frictionless surfaces have long been sought for their range of uses in mechanical engineering. Researchers are looking in the wrong places though. They should simply look at suitcase materials.

Moving carefully, I went to the back of the trolley and took hold of the handlebar. With the way ahead clear, I gave it a gentle push. The trolley didn't move.

I pushed harder until my feet were set on the concrete and my face glowed with strain. Without warning, the trolley released its stored energy and shot sideways.

The luggage leapt in all directions as if still alive. I gathered the cases up, cast a baleful glare at the trolley and left it to snare its next victim.

The air inside the terminal felt like it had been captured on some distant mountain vista, shipped here at great expense and then recycled until the musk of traveller's frustration formed a shell around every molecule.

The pale woman wandered ahead of me as I negotiated my way across the terminal's endless carpet. As I trudged, I concluded that the only possible reason for making airport terminals so large was to give you the sense that you were already getting away from it all. The drawback was that *it all* included the check-in counter that shimmered like a mirage on the distant horizon.

Reaching the shining desk, I unloaded my luggage.

"Good morning, my name is Earnest. Thank you for choosing Zephyr Zippelins for your journey today."

"Crowfat," I said absently as I handed my ticket and passport over to the man behind the counter.

"I'm sorry?" Earnest's visage glowed with his eagerness to deliver exceptional customer service.

"*Crowfat's Dilection of Customer Relations*. It's a vocal style for interactions when working in the service industry. It is supposed to make you appear helpful and fully capable of adding some joy to the receiver's day. In fact, it just makes you seem like an insufferable zygote."

"I'm not sure I—" Earnest's teeth shone brighter than the polished counter.

I set the largest of my suitcases on the scales. The weighing machine didn't whimper, so I took that as a good sign. "Dalmatian Hyperbole concluded that Crowfat was in fact tone-deaf, so he wasn't really the right person to be pioneering verbal communication techniques."

A slot in the counter purred and produced a coded luggage slip like a mottled tongue.

"Vista Class, Modicum of Comfort, or Express Transit?" Earnest asked, doing a backflip into more familiar territory.

"What's the difference?" I slipped the adhesive luggage tag through the handle of the suitcase and lined up the two sticky sides perfectly. Pressing them together meant they were no longer aligned, and I worried that I would lose my luggage without ever knowing what had been packed for me.

The suitcase slid onto a conveyor belt, and I repeated the process with the rest of my bags while Earnest explained the seating options.

"Vista Class gives you access to the glorious sky view without having to leave your seat. Express Transit gives you speedy access to the aisle for off-boarding."

"Modicum of Comfort?"

"That's the middle seat."

"I'll take the window please."

"Vista Class?"

"Yes, the window seat."

"Vista Class." Earnest said as if it were a secret handshake required to unlock the machine that printed my boarding pass.

He handed over the freshly generated page and pointed west, "Gate seventy-nine."

My luggage had vanished through the wall, so I started the long hike past everyone else.

I found Drakeforth trying on sunglasses at a stand that also sold newspapers, magazines, and apple core futures.

"Where did you get the hat?" I asked.

"I'll pick it up on my trip to the Aardvark Archipelago."

"When did you go to the Aardvarks?"

"Yes," Drakeforth replied. He paid for the sunglasses using cash, which took some convincing and finished his spending spree by going short on a three-month future contract for pickled apple cores with a fifteen per cent margin.

"Here." He handed me a hat and dark glasses similar to his own, and yet not so similar that we might be mistaken for a couple, for which I was grateful.

"You want me to wear this?"

"No, I want you to take care of it. Feed and clothe it. See it is educated and stays out of trouble with the law."

I put the hat on my head.

Drakeforth continued, "Only to one day, leave you and go out on its own to join a fringe cult of astronomers."

"Astronomers are not a fringe cult," I said, checking my look with the dark glasses in the stall mirror.

"Tell that to the people who believe that the curvature of the planet is an illusion."

"Are we in disguise? I mean, I'm not sure we are notorious enough to require disguising."

"Notoriety notwithstanding, Pudding, we are dressing appropriately for our culture. We shall arrive in Pathia, the locals will see us wearing our hats, dark glasses and perplexed expressions. Thus, they will know we are tourists and avoid us."

"Like those venomous caterpillars that are brightly coloured to warn predators that they aren't good eating?"

"Pudding, does it ever bother you that your perspective on the world is entirely limited by what you believe?"

"Nope," I cocked my hat at a jaunty angle and we started walking again through the cavernous terminal. "We have to get to gate seventy-nine."

Drakeforth gave an implied shrug.

"No rush, they won't leave without us."

"Why? Do you have the keys or something?"

Drakeforth nodded.

"Noteworthy sarcasm, Pudding."

"Gate twelve…" I commented as we passed a sign. "Gate twelve?

How many days' walk do you think it is to gate seventy-nine?"

"There was a time when I, that is, Arthur, walked all day, every day," Drakeforth mused.

"Now you just talk all day, every day?" I felt I was getting the hang of sarcasm.

"Imagine I am patting you on the head and saying, who's a good girl?"

"Is she coming with us?" I asked.

"Who?"

"That woman who has been following me around all morning."

"Well that certainly narrows it down. Is she wearing some kind of tag? *Hello, My Name Is: The Woman Following Pudding Around All Morning*?"

"I'm serious, Drakeforth. I'm having the oddest kind of day."

"Well, you are uniquely qualified to determine the oddness quotient of a given day."

I looked around as we walked. The pale woman with black hair had vanished.

"Seventy-nine," Drakeforth announced as we reached the next gate sign.

"Really? You're sure it's not forty-six with the sign turned upside down and... the number four scratched up a bit?"

"Time and space do not follow the same rules in airport terminals as they do in other time-space continuums."

I raised an eyebrow so high that if my face had been a flagpole, it would have proudly flown as the banner for cynicism.

"Why do you think these terminals are always so bandicooting large?" Drakeforth asked.

My immediate response was vetoed by an executive order from my rational mind to actually consider the question. "Well... I... I mean they have lots of zippelins to load people on to."

"Zippelins, Pudding? Zippelins take off and land vertically. They are gleaming, cone-tipped cylinders of shiny metal. When the wings are folded in, they can be parked next to each other close enough to hold a human hair between them."

"Yes, but they need space for the luggage transfer and to manage the flow of people."

"Do you have any idea how luggage is transferred from the check-in counter to the baggage carousel at your destination?"

"Of course I do! It's a system of conveyor belts and luggage handlers. You see them driving those little trucks about with the trailers all loaded up with bags."

Drakeforth gave one of his shark's-tooth smiles.

"Are you certain?"

"Yes?" I mentally rolled my eyes at my own foolishness.

"You put your luggage on one of those weighing machines, yes?"

"Yes." Like the elastic band on a cheap pair of knee-high stockings, I could see defeat coming and just kept on sliding down into rumpled discomfort.

"It went on the conveyor belt thing and vanished through a hole in the wall?"

"Yes." I sighed. Drakeforth was infuriating in the way he drew out explanations. The only thing that made it worse was the explanations were utterly ludicrous and yet, somehow plausible.

"You never see your luggage again, until it appears through another hole in the wall in some other time and space."

"Perhaps I could come back when you have finished explaining and be impressed?"

"No, Pudding. This is important. The truth of it is that no one knows where your luggage goes. Airport terminals have a strange effect on the quantum state of matter and energy. Time and space don't like to talk about it."

"So why are the terminals so large?"

"Because the larger the terminal is, the less likely you are to lose your luggage. It has been theorised that the null-space of a terminal void allows for the extrapolation of all the possible outcomes of every single state of matter."[1]

"Then why aren't there suitcases drifting around everywhere? They should be popping in and out of existence all around us."

---

1 You might want to bookmark this bit. It is going to be important in the fifth book in the Drakeforth series.

"No one can explain why, Pudding. Simply put, you don't have to believe the Universe is a cat to know nature abhors a vacuum cleaner."

"How is that putting it simply?"

Drakeforth had abandoned the conversation for the boarding gate. I joined the queue behind him, a sense of unease crinkling the skin between my shoulder blades.

I scanned the code on my boarding pass and walked through the door, the strange sensation of transience that rippled through me probably was just nerves.

CHAPTER 5

There is a reason no one writes poetry about the majestic beauty of the inside of commercial aircraft. It is the same reason why there are entire verses dedicated to the vision of birds soaring majestically as the masters of flight and not even a dirty limerick about the *inside* of those same creatures.

Much like the interior of your standard bird, the inside of a zippelin is cramped, humid, and if you are simply passing through, quite uncomfortable.

Habeas also liked to watch the zippelins coming and going. These vast silver cylinders, over a hundred feet long with aerodynamically tapered ends, moved like clouds as the reflected light of the afternoon eferncesun bounced off the paper-thin alloy shell that encased the gas bubble and passenger cabin. He watched as a loaded zippelin rose from its boarding gate mooring. It floated upwards like a soap bubble borne on the warm breath of a child's delight. With a perfect delicacy, the balloon manoeuvred into position for the flight to distant Pathia. Once the craft was pointed in the right direction, the jet engines rotated into a flight position. A moment later the empathic generators engaged the power and the sleek, silver bullet accelerated towards its destination at a velocity quickly approaching the speed of sound.

Habeas sighed; in his mind, the zippelin was the perfect combination of faith and technology. Watching these behemoths vanish over the horizon in a blur filled his heart with a righteous joy.

Going from a stationary position, to within touching distance of the speed of sound in the space of a heartbeat, comes as a surprise to many organs in the human body. The foam of the seats and the soft cuddle of the passenger harnesses held us in a comforting embrace as the air outside blurred.

We angled up into the air and then levelled off. I swallowed a wave of nausea as the rollercoaster of take-off put my spleen through a rigorous wash cycle.

With a slow breath, I looked out the window and tried to make sense of the blobs of colour passing underneath us.

The hazy sprawl of the city gave way to the smears of satellite towns, the blurred lines of highways, the green splat of forests and the smudge of ocean water.

For all its eye-watering speed, zippelin travel is one of the safest modes of transport. The safety features engineered into the navigation systems and engines of the flying machines were so complex that there were rumoured instances of an Empathic Singularity. In theory, when so many separate empathically empowered circuits were working together they could achieve a kind of awareness. Until recently, I would have rejected the idea with a sinus-clearing snort.

Experience is a great teacher. Personally, I always prefer it to be backed up by a good lesson plan and a multi-choice exam. Closing my eyes against the kaleidoscope of the landscape far below, I tried to relax and pretend I could sleep through the flight.

It started as an itch, almost a vibration rising up through the dense pressure foam of the seat. By the time it scaled my spine and brushed my teeth, it was an audible chorus of whispers. *Wheeee…!*

"Wee?" I muttered, and opened my eyes.

"Bathrooms are at the rear of the aircraft," Drakeforth replied without looking up from his magazine.

I leaned over the currently empty central seat. "Can you hear someone going, *wheee*, Drakeforth?"

"Toilet humour, Pudding?"

"What? No. I can hear voices. They're all going, *Wheeee!*"

"With an empathic resonance sensitivity like yours, Pudding, I'm surprised you don't hear more things."

"But why *wheeee*?"

Drakeforth put down his magazine. He'd been scribbling notes in one of the articles and doodling derisive faces on certain passages he had underlined. "You are in a constructed shell of metal, plastic, and empathically powered technology, hurtling through the atmosphere close to the speed of sound."

I nodded. My frown remained fixed.

"I wouldn't start worrying until you hear the voices say 'Oops'."

I sat back; Drakeforth's words made an odd kind of sense. I was picking up on the collective resonance of a legion of tiny empathically powered circuits and components. Collectively they shared a basic awareness of hurtling through the air, so why shouldn't they be enjoying themselves?

Since meeting Vole Drakeforth, the man who claimed to be the retired god of the world's foremost religion, Arthurianism, my life had been interesting. My inner critic piped up to insist that life had been quite interesting enough before Drakeforth dragged me into his lunatic conspiracy theory about the secret origins of double-e flux, the mysterious energy that ran everything. It was tempting to overlook the fact that Drakeforth's conspiracy theory was correct. The truth still made my skin crawl.

I hadn't had a lot of time to come to terms with my sensitivity to empathic resonance that was off the charts. I had always liked charts. They brought order to chaos and represented large volumes of data in clear terms that could often foresee the future better than reading tea leaves.

Not being dead just made things more complicated.

I think being dead would have removed a great deal of responsibility. Of course I didn't have enough experience of being dead to say for sure.

Arthurians tended to scoff at questions about death. To them, there is an acceptable level of probability that we are energy and energy cannot be created or destroyed. Energy can be *inconvenienced* by being forced into the shape of a bored youth serving burgers in any one of the faceless corporate franchise outlets. However, with perseverance and the passing of puberty, even energy can make something of itself and finally transform into a form far less aggravating.

I once had a T-shirt with a quote attributed to the Arthurian physicist, Toronomy Snoot, printed on it: *"Energy is an Optimist."*

Once I would have said that attributing any kind of world view to something as elemental as energy was simply an effect of empathic resonance. Now, I wasn't so sure. Every vibrating particle and wave of double-e flux was once part of a person. A life lived and experience gained. Now, like the individual fibres that make up the yarn that is woven into a pullover, some tiny fragment of those lives had been diverted into empathic energy and was being used to send us hurtling through the air. *Wheee!* indeed.

The worst part is that the constant drone of delight made sleeping away the long hours of the flight impossible.

The inflight service menu sounded delicious. After our food arrived, I concluded the same person who named our seats wrote the menu.

Sense Media systems on zippelins have limited immersion, something about the unpleasant effect of being fully engaged in a four-dimensional sensory reality when hitting turbulence. The novelty of watching a sensie on a 2D screen wore off quickly.

In a fit of terminal boredom, I ended up reading a travel guide to Pathia.

Pathia, the guidebook said (thanks to the audio function and complimentary headphones) is an ancient country, steeped in tradition and a rich cultural history.

My experience of other countries was limited, though I felt sure a rich cultural heritage meant your grandparents grew up without the benefits of indoor plumbing.

Accepted by Arthurian scholars to be the area where Arthur

himself first began the religion that bears his name, modern Pathia has no formal religion and is considered one of the most secular countries in the world.

I looked over towards the aisle, intending to ask Drakeforth if this was true. The pale woman was back in the seat between us and once again, I hadn't noticed her leave or return.

She had her knees up against her chin and her feet flat on the edge of the narrow seat. She wiggled her alabaster toes like the sensory papilla of some exotically anaemic sea slug.

"Who are you?" I asked. She turned her head, a wave of black silk hair cascading past her face in a way that if I wasn't seeing it for myself, I would say was computer generated.

"Seriously," I added.

In response, she lifted a single finger to her lips and made a silent, *shh* gesture. I shivered.

"Drakeforth?"

"Vole isn't here right now. Would you like to leave a message?" he replied from the aisle seat.

"Do you know this person?" I nodded significantly at the strange woman seated between us.

"Do any of us really know anyone?" Drakeforth replied. I leaned forward. He had his hat brim pulled down over his eyes.

"This is important," I insisted.

"Importance is all a matter of perspective." He was talking into his hat.

"Well, apply some perspective to the person sitting in the seat between us," I snapped.

Drakeforth pushed the brim of his hat upwards with one finger. His eyes rolled in my direction and then rolled away again.

"I think this is my stop," he announced. Before I could comment, Drakeforth had left his seat and vanished up the narrow aisle towards the bar at the front of the passenger cabin.

"I could make a career out of apologising for him," I said. "Maybe write a book. Like a manual or a user guide or something. Do lecture tours and run seminars at tropical resorts." I let this daydream run for a few more seconds and started thinking that no matter how lucrative the idea, it would involve addressing large groups of strangers. I went back to my book.

By the time we were asked to stow our tray tables, return our seats to the upright position, and engage our 8-point inertia-dampening harnesses in preparation for landing, the book assured me that I had learned everything there was to know about Pathia.

Sand. The country was the world's largest litter box. Cats were an integral part of Pathia's history and culture, and the country's borders were defined by water on three sides and a mountain range on the other two.

All that sand made for a changing landscape, which is why the Pathians had invented geometry and cartography before other primitive technology like the wheel and the humorous greeting card. The guidebook had an entire chapter about early attempts to make maps that would show land ownership. It was two centuries before the concept of scale was invented and maps were no longer required to be actual size.

Aside from the general dismissal of organised religion, Pathia had given up on the idea of money. Their economy did not operate on a complex system of cheques and balances. Instead, they operated on something called the *Knowledge Economy*. It sounded impossibly confusing. I gleaned from the guidebook that the basic idea was that it wasn't the value of the product or service someone provided, but some kind of intangible value of the contribution to the knowledge and betterment of society as a whole that their economic system was based on. Pathia, the book said, is a country where information is more valuable than rare minerals.

When we landed in the capital city of Semita, I felt ready to pass any kind of immigration pop-quiz they might hit me with at customs.

CHAPTER 6

Filing out of the zippelin, the first thing that hit me was the heat. The second thing that hit me was the *heat*. Pathia baked under an eternal summer. The worst part of it was the way the heat came up from the ground; it was as hot as the sun shining down, except without the bright light.

"Hat, glasses," Drakeforth instructed. I nodded, my eyes screwed shut against the glare as I fumbled for our purchases.

It made a nice difference, and as long as I didn't breathe, the heat was merely unbearable.

"Brrr," Drakeforth shivered.

"Yes, we should get inside before we freeze to death." In the same way that vaccines trick your immune system into fighting a disease with biological props, I felt I was getting the hang of hanging with Drakeforth.

We made it to the terminal, where the doors seemed to steel themselves before opening. Inside it was cooler, with a great colour scheme and eye-catching modern art installations. The temperature was much lower than outside, too.

"Try not to let them know that you know," Drakeforth murmured.

"Who? What?"

"Exactly." Drakeforth nodded.

If we were going to be tourists, that meant souvenirs. I went to a nearby shop selling T-shirts and flipped through the racks.

Drakeforth stood back and watched her shop.

"Pudding, we are at a junction in what, for simplicity's sake, we will call space and time. You are going to make the first of many choices. The outcome of those choices, of course, will remain unknown to you until it is far too late. You will know about this later because you are going to write it all down, or he will. And if you think that's breaking the fourth wall, then just you wait till I break the fifth wall."[1]

My credit stick still worked in this part of the world, which was a relief. I held up a T-shirt for Drakeforth to see.

"My Sister Went to Pathia and All I Got Was This Amazing T-shirt," I read. "I got it for Ascott. He hates souvenirs."

"I'm sure he will not love it," Drakeforth replied.

We joined the queue of people seeking formal admission to the country. While we waited to be admitted, I wondered: If we weren't in Pathia in the official sense, then where the herbivore were we?

My passport got stamped by an immigration official with long hair in a complex sculpted style that suggested he used wallpaper paste as shampoo and slept on it wet.

I followed the signs to the baggage claim area and stood in expectant silence among a hundred other people, all of us staring at the luggage conveyor and waiting for the obvious to happen.

There are people who devote their lives to studying the big mysteries. They are motivated by money, curiosity, boredom, or, in many cases, the overwhelming need to prove that they are right, and everyone who ever doubted them can go do what famous playwright, Colin Oscopy, once invited the *East Geshun Observer*'s critic to do with her first night review of the production of Colin's new play, *Aubergine Emergent*.

When people converge in groups around airport baggage claims, I am reminded that someone, for some reason, designed the entire baggage retrieval system in a certain way. I'm equally certain, that, like Oscopy, they harboured a deep, irrational hatred against their fellow man.

---

1 Breaking the fourth wall is when a character in the story addresses the audience directly. The fifth wall is when you get taken out of the story by realising that someone is reading over your shoulder. Aimee hates it when people do that.

After forty minutes, Drakeforth joined me, a steaming take-away cup of tea in his hand. "Having fun?" he asked.

"Gosh, yes!" I gushed. "I saw all these other people standing around and I thought, that looks like the sort of mind-numbing activity I would really enjoy, and you know what? It's more wonderfully mind-numbing than I ever imagined it would be."

"Your bags are over there." Drakeforth indicated a trolley so similar to the one I had wrestled with at the beginning of our journey that I wondered, for a moment, if we had ever left our point of departure.

"Right…" I took a deep breath and let my shoulders drop. "Where have you been for the last forty minutes?"

Drakeforth raised his take-away cup, "I've been sitting over there drinking tea, enjoying a fresh scone and wondering what you were doing standing at the baggage claim."

"Pathia is a desert country, isn't it?"

"Mostly," Drakeforth agreed.

"Lots of loose soil, easy digging?"

"In places."

I looked around. "I wonder if I can buy a shovel here? Or some other tool suitable for digging a shallow grave."

"In Pathia, traditionally the dead are not buried, they are pathed."

"Passed?" I frowned.

"No, after they have passed, they are pathed."

I reached for my guidebook and thumbed through it until I found the section on burial customs. I read in silence for a few moments.

"Oh, you have got to be kidding!"

"Mind where you step," Drakeforth said. "And when you see a sign saying, *Keep On The Grass*, do it."

Between the city of Semita and us, a young woman with short hair stood holding a sign. In local pictograms and carefully printed letters, it said: *Experienced Pathologist. Reasonable Daily Rates.*

A cat was weaving between her bare ankles in a figure eight pattern that seemed to generate bliss for the small creature and made my toes curl in ticklish empathy.

Drakeforth went and spoke with her, and then leaned in and whispered something in her ear. They shook hands and she introduced herself as Harenae, and immediately offered to drive our trolley.

"Be my guest."

I didn't think it was fair to inflict Drakeforth and an airport trolley on her on the same day. However, she guided the trolley across the terminal with a casual ease that made my eyes narrow. The cat groomed itself and watched us leave.

CHAPTER 7

"Archaeology, Pudding. Ever taken a fancy to it?" Drakeforth asked.

"You mean the study of human history and prehistory through the excavation of sites and the analysis of artefacts and other physical remains?"

"I was thinking more the marine zoo construction, but sure, let's go with your version."

"It's never been a passion. On account of all the dirt."

"Most of the world is made of dirt."

"And yet the oceans get all the credit," I agreed.

"Better coverage," Drakeforth said.

"You have until we reach the exit to this terminal to make your point, Drakeforth."

"Archaeology was invented in Pathia."

"On account of all the dirt, no doubt."

"It's a fine thought, Pudding. However, the accepted theory is because Pathia has a long and continuous history of civilisation. Which means there is a lot of it to dig up."

"Convenient. Much like that exit…"

Leaving the terminal building, I readied myself for the wave of heat; what took me by surprise was the smell of drifting smoke.

"Is there a fire?" I asked our guide.

"Pathia doesn't use empathic energy the way other countries do," Harenae explained.

"But that building, it has smoke coming out of it."

"Yes, because it is burning fuel to generate electricity," Harenae replied with the calm patience of someone who has had the same conversation with tourists many times before.

"Isn't that, well, a fire hazard?"

"Yes," she nodded. "If it wasn't, it wouldn't work."

Where I expected to see cars, instead I saw people. Mostly they were walking, though some were riding on raised platforms carried on the shoulders of teams of athletic young people.

"I thought there would be more *Moo-rise,*" I said in an attempt to appear less inept.

Harenae continued in the same patient tone, "The spelling is *M-u-r-r-a-i,* but it is pronounced *Murray*. And yes, they are made of stone. They were the main labour force of Pathia for centuries. Murrai are the only working examples of empathically powered devices used in Pathia. Walk or ride?"

"I think we will walk," Drakeforth replied. "Destination, the Hotel Dust."

"Hotel Dust," Harenae nodded and whistled at three men huddled in the shade. They came over and picked up our luggage.

"Hotel Dust," she said to the three porters. They squared their shoulders, wiped their feet on the smooth stone, and headed off with our bags. We fell into step behind Harenae and the luggage bearers.

"Are all the roads in Pathia made the same way?" I asked Drakeforth.

"Many of them are made from local quarried stone. There was a time when all construction work was done by murrai, but they're less common these days."

"Then, we're not actually walking on people?"

Drakeforth did the thing where he walks in a straight line while turning his head to regard me with his unique blend of contempt and curiosity. It would have been more annoying, if he hadn't made it look effortless.

"Pathia, means *the place of paths,*" he said. "However, unless we are walking on an osteopath, then it is unlikely that we are walking on human remains."

"Of course." I tried to snort, but the air was very dry so it came out as more of a whistle. "That would make Harenae a pathologist?"

"Yes," Drakeforth turned his attention back to the way ahead.

We walked on smooth stones, a mosaic jigsaw of well-fitted pieces that, the more I stared at it, the more it hinted at a pattern. Some kind of structure, perhaps a written language in letters too large or ancient to be understood.

"Don't look down," Harenae announced.

"Hmm?" I replied with a sliver of attention.

"Look ahead, above or behind, never down. You might see something you like."

"I can almost make out...something."

"The secrets of the path are not for our eyes. They are all that remains of the ancient world. Well, that and the murrai, the pyramids, and the museum archives."

"The pyramids? Oh yes, I read about those," I said brightly, still not wanting to appear like a complete tourist.

"You read what was in the guide books," Harenae said. Her lack of confidence clear.

"Uhh, yes?" I could almost hear Drakeforth rolling his eyes.

Harenae continued, "Don't stare at the stones, or the gaps between them. They came from ancient pyramids; we call it crazy paving because those who stare too long go pyramad."

"Pyramad?"

"It's a well-documented mental condition," Drakeforth said.

"Okay..." I glanced once more at the pattern of lines between the stones and wrenched my eyes away.

We walked along a winding path between buildings made of sand-coloured stone. This is what sand castles must look like to a crab crossing the beach between tides.

The Hotel Dust—a tower of sand coloured blocks with a hanging sign of mummified wood creaking in the breeze. The only recognisable part of the sign were the five stars, faded, cracked and all but two had been scratched out.

A stencilled image in fresh red paint on one wall looked like a credit stick. I wondered why, as I hadn't seen any terminals for making electronic transactions outside the airport.

"Your destination," Harenae said. The porters lifted our luggage down and smiled at me, their hands outstretched, palms up.

Drakeforth slipped a folded, handwritten note into each empty hand, which struck me as weird, but the locals smiled and nodded.

"We'll send word if we require your services again," he said.

Harenae nodded and followed the porters as they marched off into the sweltering heat.

I followed Drakeforth into the cool, cave-like interior of the hotel.

CHAPTER 8

"Two rooms, with working air-conditioning and windows. Preferably ones that close," Drakeforth explained to the long-haired youth behind the stone block that served as a counter. Two cats lounged in the only chairs available in the guest side of the reception area, their expressions suggesting the faded cushions would only be pried from their cold, dead paws.

"How many nights?" The youth sounded male. It surprised me: in the gloom I had assumed he was a girl.

"Let's not make assumptions," Drakeforth replied.

"We have one room available, it's the honeymoon suite."

"Oh, we're not—" I said quickly.

Drakeforth took a pencil and scrap of paper from his pocket. He wrote something on it and slid it over the counter.

"Here's an idea," he said. The young man glanced down and took the paper, leaving the key unattended as he swept the note out of sight.

"Bring the bags," Drakeforth said, as he started up a flight of stone steps.

The youth and I cycled through an eternity of not making eye contact, then glancing at each other questioningly, then feeling awkward until I grabbed one of my suitcases and headed it up the stairs.

"It's all right," I said to Drakeforth when I found him on the third floor. "I'll get the bags."

"I'm glad I didn't have to ask twice," Drakeforth replied.

I put the case down and went back downstairs to collect the

others. In the lobby, a discussion was warming rapidly. I stopped just out of sight and listened.

"He always stays here." A woman's voice.

"No one chooses to stay here," the boy behind the stone counter replied.

"Vole Drakeforth is a creature of habit. Many of them quite inexplicable, but it does make him predictable."

Not wanting to be caught eavesdropping, I stepped down and picked up two more suitcases.

"Cacolet-leather," the woman said.

I mentally sighed. "Yes."

"Are you here with Vole?"

"That would depend on who wants to know."

She wore a loose robe of pale green cloth that draped and twisted, giving her the appearance of being woven into the centre of some archaic knot. Her skin was tanned, but her eyes and hair were as light as the sand. However, unlike the sand, her eyes were blue.

"I told him to come," she said.

"Ah." I lifted the suitcases and started up the stairs.

"You don't believe me?" she said to my back.

"Quite right."

I heard the scuff of her feet on the stone steps behind me as I stepped around a cat escorting me up the stairs.

"Drakeforth never does anything anyone tells him," I explained.

"Well, he listens to me," she said as we climbed past the second floor.

"You must have something serious to blackmail him with," I replied.

"Oh, it's nothing like that. I'm his wife."

CHAPTER 9

After we climbed to the third floor, I sat down on the top step. "Wife?" I repeated.

"Yes, it's complicated. We aren't together in the normal sense. In fact, the entire marriage was simply so I could work here in Pathia."

"A marriage of convenience?"

"A marriage of *in*convenience. We had to live together for a year to prove it wasn't an immigration scam."

"But…it was?"

"Totally."

Questions jostled in my mind trying to get to the head of the queue. I picked one at random.

"What sort of work do you do?"

She sat down on the step next to me and spoke quietly. "I'm an archaeologist."

"Oh. Marine zoo construction or fossicking in the dirt for ancient history?"

"*Shhh…*" she hushed me, and looked around the empty staircase. "Not so loud. There are some very strict rules about history in Pathia. Officially, I'm a librarian at the Museum of Pathia."

"That sounds interesting…" I worked on breathing. The zip-lag, sweatbox temperatures, and strange revelations had combined to leave me weak and light-headed.

"It's more interesting than studying economic modelling forecasts based on consideration of factors culminating in alternative outcomes to historically valid events."

My memory latched on to the strangely familiar that bobbed to the surface on the shifting tide. "Beaufort College…"

"Vole and I met there as students," the woman in green replied.

"Was he insufferable in those days?" I rested my head against the wall; the warmth and texture of it made me feel like I was leaning against a sleeping armadillo.

"Vole was…difficult. Fiercely intelligent and utterly helpless. He spent far too much time in the local teahouses. If I hadn't tutored him, he would have dropped out."

"He never mentioned you."

"He never mentioned you, either," she replied.

"Charlotte Pudding." I extended a pale hand.

"Eade Notschnott." We shook on it.

Eade helped with the luggage and, with an unsettling confidence, went directly to the Honeymoon Suite, Room 3.14. Drakeforth was inside, on his hands and knees, tapping the stone block that made the bed base, a frown of concentration on his face.

"Still solid?" Eade asked as she set my luggage down.

"Notschnott, have you met Pudding?"

"Yes, Vole we've met."

I came in and closed the door in my wake. I set the last of the bags down and through the film of sweat evaporating from my eyes, I saw a refrigerator. I went to it and found bottles of water chilled to perfection. I drank one and took three more with me to where Eade was watching Drakeforth continue his crawl around the room's only bed.

"Water?" I offered one of the bottles.

"Thank you." She took it and saluted me with the bottle before taking a long drink.

"Will he be long, do you think?" I asked as I sipped my second bottle of ice water.

"It would help to pass the time if I explain."

"It's really not necessary."

"It would help *me* pass the time," Eade clarified. "Vole Drake-forth has some issues."

I gave a snort. "He's like a weekly magazine with legs."

"Exactly."

"I can hear you, you know," Drakeforth said from the other side of the bed.

"Of course you can." Eade managed to avoid sounding totally condescending. I was impressed.

Eade continued to talk to me as if Drakeforth were not present. "His current concern relates to the truth about the double-e flux known as empathic energy; he has some strange ideas about where the Godden Corporation gets its source material from."

I brightened. "Oh yes, we had that adventure. Turns out that Drakeforth was right to be concerned. The Godden Corporation are harvesting the essence of the living to capture the empathic energy that they then use to power everything."

"Vole, you were actually right about something?" Eade sounded surprised.

"Yes," Drakeforth snapped.

"Well done, you should write that down somewhere. Perhaps note it in your diary so you can celebrate the anniversary of the day you got something right."

Drakeforth stood up.

"Yes," he said, dusting his hands off. "Yes. I should do that."

I expected Drakeforth to unleash his particularly biting sarcasm, finely honed in the depths of the Sarkazian Clubs where sarcasm was practised with the intensity and devastating effect of a martial art.

"You're probably wondering why I insisted you come at once," Eade continued.

It was Drakeforth's turn to give Eade his full attention for the first time: "There is only one reason you would contact me and insist I come back to Pathia. Either you have found something, or you have lost something. No one ever enlists the help of others when they find something. Therefore, you have lost something. Given that we are in Pathia, it's probably something that you can't tell anyone in authority about. Something you were responsible for, which means it is an Arthurian artefact."

Eade shook her head. "That would be ridiculous. This crisis

is far bigger than library robbery." She took a deep breath. "Professor Bombilate is missing."

"Good," Drakeforth replied.

"Good? Good? Are you completely deranged? The professor goes missing and all you can say is *good*?"

"I could say, great, outstanding. Wonderful and about bingo time."

Eade turned on me. "Has Vole suffered any recent blows to the head that you know of?"

I did a quick mental count. "Several."

Drakeforth raised a hand to stop Eade as she stepped forward, hands raised ready to examine his skull. "My brain is fine. A great deal has happened since you and I last saw each other, Notschnott. You should know, I got religion."

"Oh, Vole!" Eade pressed her palm against Drakeforth's forehead, as if checking him for a fever.

"He's not sick," I said. "At least, not like that. Drakeforth is Arthur."

"Water, quickly," Eade waved a hand at me as she pushed Drakeforth into a sitting position on the edge of the bed. I handed over a bottle. Eade twisted the lid off and threw the contents in Drakeforth's face.

"Snap out of it, for mango's sake!" she shouted.

"Fargarble!" Drakeforth shouted. He stood up and swept water off his face. "For once in your life, would you just listen?" he demanded.

"Why? Are you finally going to say something worth listening to?" Eade retorted.

"Yes! Probably! I—Oh, never mind…"

At its core, capitalism is about bridging the gap between the customer (the mark with the money) and the guy wanting to unburden them of all that credit. Customer service is the nice arch over the bottomless chasm that makes the customer appreciate the bridge as something more than a piece of clever engineering. With this in mind, I took a deep breath.

"Would it help if I explained?"

"Probably not," Drakeforth replied.

"Go on then," Eade said, regarding me as if I was a puppy being encouraged to perform a trick.

"Drakeforth was right. About everything. I don't know how or why, but he is also Arthur, the founder and actual god of Arthurianism. Honestly, if you thought he was odd before, you should hang out with him for an hour and then we can compare notes."

"Well, that answers that question," Eade said.

"Which question?" I asked warily.

"The *'Have I called upon the right person in my time of greatest need?'* question. The answer is clearly *no*."

"We are here now, so you may as well make the best of it," Drakeforth said.

"Professor Bombilate?" I suggested.

"What?" Eade blinked. "Oh! Yes, Professor Bombilate is missing.

"Have you checked between the sofa cushions?" I said, with a fixed expression of calm.

Eade gave me a pitying look.

"Who is Professor Bombilate?" I said, feeling my face redden.

"Professor Bombilate is the world's leading informist," Eade replied.

"What is—?" I stopped as Drakeforth raised a hand.

"Pathia has a knowledge-based economy, Pudding. You did read the guide book, didn't you?"

"Well, yes. I mean, I listened to the audio version and I have used it for reference a couple of times."

"In Pathia, an informist analyses the value of, and tracks the ups and downs of, the economy, exactly as an economist does back home. Except instead of shares, products, services, interest rates, employment figures and apple-core futures, an informist analyses the flow and changing value of information."

"So how do people pay for things?"

"By the sharing of information."

I had a flash of understanding. "There was something written on the paper you gave the porters and you whispered something to Harenae, the guide. You were paying them for their services."

Eade applauded. "Aren't you clever? Vole, give her a treat."

"Most of the world's economies are based on scarcity," Drakeforth continued. "Living Oak, for example, was used as a currency for a while, because it was rare and considered valuable, so people hoarded it like gold. Information, on the other hand, is abundant. It's like trying to base your economy on units of air."

"Which is only important if you're not getting any," I said, and realised that there was a second line to that joke, but I had messed up the delivery. "Uhm…"

"Information is exactly the same," Drakeforth nodded. "People always believe that there is something essential they do not know. It's like a fish worrying that they don't have enough water. Or a billipede counting its feet."

"So…the perception of scarcity, even in the abundance of information, is what gives it variable value?" I was relieved that Eade remained silent. I took it to mean I had made a decent contribution to the conversation.

"Sure, why not?" Drakeforth shrugged. "It's also because Pathians have developed a finely tuned and well-functioning economy based on the idea of an idea. Now it's so entrenched that they can't for a moment consider that it's all ridiculous because then the entire place would collapse into chaos overnight."

"But that's true for most… Oh…" I fell silent. There are some things that people aren't meant to look at too closely. Ideas and the systems that keep everything ticking along, the lights on, and the bills paid, are among them.

Drakeforth nodded at my realisation. "There are some abysses that you shouldn't stare too long into. If you do, then they stare back, and you start wondering if they are staring at you, or if it's someone behind you. Then you might think you should say something, or is it that the abyss said something and you didn't hear it? The important thing is to remember, that way lies asparagus."

"Asparagus…?" I whispered.

"Best avoided," Drakeforth nodded.

I mentally grabbed the steering wheel and did a handbrake

turn on the conversation, "I saw a sign on a wall. It looked like a credit stick."

"Where?" Eade asked sharply.

"In the street, outside the hotel."

"Lore Officers will remove it. It's the symbol of a terrorist group. They call themselves *The Credit Union*."

I waited in silence, determined not to ask the stupid question for once.

Eade looked disappointed. "The CU want Pathia to abandon the knowledge economy and adopt the more universal credit system. Electronic banking in the form of digital currency, rather than the more tangible knowledge that is currently used.

"They are considered a terrorist organisation because their ideas are potentially disruptive to the economy and society as a whole."

"Do they blow up buildings or kidnap people?" I asked.

"No, but they are growing in influence, and more people are starting to consider their ideas."

"Maybe they kidnapped Professor Bombilate?"

"Maybe they didn't," Drakeforth said.

"Oooh… That would make a great conspiracy theory. They didn't actually kidnap Professor Bombilate. They just want everyone to think they did."

"They have a lot to answer for," Drakeforth agreed.

"It was more fun when I didn't know who they were," I said with a sudden pang of seriousness.

"It was joyous when they didn't know who we were," Drakeforth said dryly.

Neither of us had noticed that Eade had left.

Drakeforth sighed and suddenly smiled. "Sofa cushions." He chuckled in a way that sounded like someone who had never chuckled before thought it should sound. "That was good."

CHAPTER 10

"She was here, wasn't she? I didn't imagine it?" Hysteria wasn't included in any of the verbal communication styles I had studied, so I told myself that I wasn't being hysterical. Adamant? Certainly. Insistent? Definitely. Weeping and gibbering? Not on your life!

"Who?" Drakeforth asked.

"Eade Notschnott?" I said.

"Yes. Eade has left the building."

"What did you mean, *who*?"

"I meant Eade, obviously." Drakeforth's gaze skittered across my face like an eel on ice-skates.

"Of course," I nodded, and looked around the room. The dark-haired woman had been inconspicuously absent since we left the terminal. Not knowing where she might be made my skin crawl.

Drakeforth rubbed his hands together.

"Right then. When you are ready, we should get on with it."

"Let's assume that I will be ready by the time you have finished explaining exactly what *it* is," I replied, and opened my first suitcase.

"Professor Bombilate. Informist. Missing. Eade needs us to find him. Or at least, find out why he can't be found."

I hung a colourful dress in the closet provided.

"Yes, I heard. Where do you find someone who isn't where they expect to be?"

"A wise woman once said anything lost is always found in the

47

last place you look, so look there first."

"The trick is knowing where the last place to look is," I suggested.

"Probably," Drakeforth almost agreed. He sat down on the edge of the bed and with the sudden determination of someone leaping off a building in the fervent belief they can fly, he lay down.

"You're taking a nap?" I asked, my arms folding in disapproval.

"I'm thinking," Drakeforth replied, his eyes closed.

"I'm going to take a shower," I said.

"Good for you."

I opened a door. It turned out to be a smaller closet.

"Yes, nothing like a hot shower after a long trip."

"Quite right," Drakeforth replied.

"Makes you feel like a new person…" I opened the fridge again. The lack of voice interaction from the appliance was really strange.

"Through the door to your left," Drakeforth announced.

"There's no door on that wall, I would have—Oh." Of course there was a door on the wall, just to the left of the fridge. Of course there hadn't been a door there a moment ago, either.

My experience with foreign bathrooms is limited. I had always assumed they all followed the same principle: some kind of toilet, hot and cold running water, shower nozzle, or maybe a tub with taps.

If I ignored the shower floor's resemblance to a litter box, and the larger than necessary pipe above, it could have been a bathroom. At least a modern-art installation interpretation of one.

I pulled the lever on the wall. The pipe rattled, gurgled and then coughed a cloud of fine dust. Taking a deep breath, the pipe warmed up and disgorged a flood of dust. I slapped the lever closed and the flow stopped.

Brushing myself off, I stepped out of the room.

"Very funny," I snapped.

"I thought you were taking a shower," Drakeforth said from his position on the bed.

"There's no water!"

Drakeforth opened his eyes and addressing the ceiling, said: "You're in Pathia."

"I am aware of that."

"Pathia is a desert country. There *is* no water."

"Clearly there is, I've drunk several bottles of it since we arrived in this room."

"Imported, they call it. Slavery would be a more accurate term, of course."

"Slavery?"

"Do you think anyone asked the water if it wanted to be transported half way around the world and put in bottles?"

"Well no, but it's water."

"Exactly." Drakeforth's eyes closed again.

"The shower…?" I ventured.

"In Pathia, you bathe in dust."

"Surely the point is to remove the dust?" I replied.

"Don't worry, the dirt is very clean."

Sometimes stubbornness is like a suit of armour. You put it on, even though it is uncomfortable, cumbersome, and not best suited for most day-to-day activities. You wear it to make a point.

I returned to the bathroom, hung my clothes up and turned on the dust.

"Better?" Drakeforth asked from the bed when I returned.

"I feel…oddly polished."

"We should go." Drakeforth swung his legs off the bed and stood up.

"Yes, the missing man is not going to find himself." I reached for my coat, and then remembered we were in a country where their idea of water was sand. I wondered if I should take a shovel instead. We donned our dark glasses and hats and left the hotel.

CHAPTER 11

It was still hotter outside than inside, which made going back inside something to look forward to. I followed Drakeforth through the dusty streets, carefully avoiding eye contact with the irregular paving stones.

"Yes, quite different," he said.

"What?" I hurried to catch up.

"Nothing."

"Where are we going to start our search?" I asked.

"Bombilate had an interest in forbidden things. So we will go to the source and work our way backwards or forwards from there."

"That sounds... What's the term for something that isn't lethally dangerous, but is hugely inadvisable?"

"Crocodile dentistry?"

"Not exactly what I was thinking of, but metaphorically appropriate, I suppose."

We descended into a swirling maelstrom of brightly coloured people wearing dusty clothes. They clumped together around a variety of market stalls sold a variety of food and vacuum cleaners. Most of the trading seemed to done in low murmurs, punctuated by the occasional exchange of folded notes.

I truly felt like a tourist among the natives with their loose-fitting dust-and-wear clothing. Keeping track of Drakeforth in the bustling market was easy enough: his hat and his air of general contempt for the world glowed like an aura.

Flies swarmed and buzzed around a section of the market

selling meat. I raised a hand to brush away a fly intent on examining my eyelashes. A breath of chill air raised the hairs on my neck and the dark-haired woman stood beside me. Her icy hand held my wrist in a death grip, and I gasped at the sudden shock of it. She shook her head as the fly finished its inspection and flew off to crawl on someone else.

With a deft dip she retrieved the guidebook from my bag and held it open, displaying an easy-to-follow infographic that detailed how flies are sacred in Pathia.

The punishment for the crime of striking a fly looked to be painful and messy, even rendered in clip-art icons.

"Thanks…" I whispered, looking around furtively to see if anyone had noticed my brush with the law.

"Put that away." Drakeforth pushed the book back into my bag.

"Sorry, I almost hit a fly. Apparently that would be a bad idea."

"Very bad. Worse is flashing a book around in public. It's like waving your credit stick or fanning yourself with bundles of cash."

"Oh… She's here again, the woman."

"Try to keep up, Pudding." Drakeforth took me by the arm and guided me through the crowd. We left the silent woman standing in the market, until the crowd and flies obscured her from view.

"Where are we going?" I asked. "You mentioned a forbidden place?"

"The centre of the Pathian civilisation. The single most important place in the entire country."

"An ice factory?"

"The ancient ruins of the city of Errm."

"That's the source of all forbidden things in Pathia?" I whispered.

"Exactly. It is also where we start our search for the missing informist.

"Perhaps he went to a pub?" It seemed like a long shot, but hope insisted I suggest it.

"Unlikely, though I applaud your lateral thinking, Pudding."

"Is it far, this ruined city?"

"It all depends on how you perceive distance."

"Drakeforth," I said in as sweet a voice as I could muster. "Tell me how far it actually is, or I swear, I will not rest until your name and contact details are on every Arthurian mailing list I can find."

"You wouldn't!?" Drakeforth fell silent as I smiled beatifically at him. "It's a few miles. Would you rather take a litter than walk?"

"In this heat? I would rather stay in the hotel and build an air conditioner out of toothpicks. Though if we must go, then, yes, by litter, please."

We reached the edge of the market, where it bled into the surrounding maze of narrow streets and sandcastle architecture.

Drakeforth whistled at a group of young, athletic types who were leaning against a wall, a covered platform beside them.

"Two for the ruins of Errm," Drakeforth explained.

"Whaddyaknow?" one of the youths asked, sizing us up with the contempt of the adolescent.

"I know plenty," Drakeforth replied.

"You don't say?" the youth countered.

"No, I don't. Not until it's time to pay the fare."

"From here to the ruins? That's gonna cost you."

"Well, get your litter mates and let's get moving then. Pay attention, you may earn something."

The youth nodded slowly and then jerked his head at his lolling friends. They got up and lifted the litter onto their shoulders. In a synchronised movement, they sank to one knee, positioning the litter for us to board.

"Thank you for choosing Kitteh's litter services, we believe in the human touch," the youth said in a practiced way as we took our seats under a canopy of light fabric that protected us from the glare.

I gasped, reflexively clutching Drakeforth's hand as the litter rose, and our carriers swayed under us.

"Relax, Pudding. We are on the shoulders of professionals. Besides, it's against the law to drop litter in Pathia."

CHAPTER 12

We hurried down narrow streets that linked up to wider arterial routes, where modern cars coughed like a cat bringing up a hairball as they farted a steady stream of grey smoke. My self-conscious feeling at using an archaic form of transport like a litter quickly faded with the smooth ride. We glided past the occasional traffic jam like ants with full bellies.

In the heat and dust, everyone was bustling, going about their business with an intensity that made me feel exhausted just watching it.

"Makes you think, doesn't it?" Drakeforth said.

"It does?"

"It makes me think people are really stupid."

"I think you envy regular people." I ignored Drakeforth's derisive snort and continued, "The ones who go through their entire lives, with all the normal problems that people face. The tragedies, setbacks, the ups and downs. The stuff that we all deal with. You, on the other hand, are walking around sneering down your nose at all these people who are getting on with living."

"I am not," said Drakeforth, waving my rant away.

"You've been doing that since the day we met. It's what drives you." I made a vague gesture. "This eye-rolling dismissiveness is your thing."

"You dropped something," Drakeforth said.

"What?" I looked down.

"Your argument," Drakeforth replied. "You started out with a strong attack and then completely apologised for it. You dropped it."

"Do not change the subject."

"It's frustration," Drakeforth announced.

I did a quick mental tally on the last few moments.

"Did you just change the subject back?"

"Really, Pudding, if you can't keep up, take notes."

"You're saying you don't like people because you're frustrated?"

"I'm not frustrated, people are frustrating."

I went back to watching the scenery, or at least watching the people and cars that blocked my view of the scenery.

Drakeforth sighed. I stared harder into the beige haze. There comes a point in every conversation when staying silent is the best option. According to the dialectic teachings of Master Qualtagh, all dialogue exchange is a form of combat. For Qualtagh, the one who breaks the silence first better have deleted their browser history.

Right now, I felt I could remain *shush* until the cows not only came home, but also had their dinner, watched some TV and went to bed.

A jigsaw wall of massive sandstone blocks marked the edge of the city. We passed under an archway and into the desert, which looked like the city wall, but laid on its side.

The desert looked like every picture of a desert I had ever seen, except more realistic. Our bearers bore us down the road that passed through the dunes without breaking stride.

My guidebook said trees hadn't been common in Pathia for thousands of years. Instead of trees, a hardy variety of grass grew in vast plains, eaten and fertilised by the goats herded across them. In the last few centuries, the demand for free-range goat products had declined. Without the goats to fertilise the plains, the deserts had spread. The cause of this change wasn't covered in the book, probably because it was obvious.

After an hour, the endurance of the litter bearers would have impressed anyone who hadn't spent that time with Drakeforth. Neither of us had said a word, and I was itching to say something.

Kitteh's crew came to a halt and lowered us to the ground. I eased out of the litter and stretched until I yawned.

Drakeforth exited and made a whispered transaction with Kitteh. Our carrier's eyes went wide, and he did a double take at Drakeforth. Then he went and shared his apparent good fortune with the rest of his team.

Mid-stretch, I blinked. *She* stood on a nearby dune, her hair flowing in the light breeze like dark seaweed wafting on unseen currents.

"Drakeforth, look!" I blurted.

"Ha!" he whooped and slapped his thigh.

"*Gargle!*" I swore. "Look! It's that woman again."

"You lose!" Drakeforth crowed. "Lose-*her!*"

"Yes, you are very clever. Now pay attention, *drammi*t."

"Personally, I think Qualtagh was just socially awkward and terribly shy. But he is popular with devotees of dialectics, so I knew you were waiting for me to say something."

I paid half an ear to Drakeforth, my focus on the dune where the strange woman had just disappeared. "Well done, Drakeforth. You may have a cookie."

Drakeforth seemed satisfied that his victory was complete. Hands on his hips, he surveyed the endless sea of dust. "Some people," he declared, "upon finding themselves lost in the desert, would embrace the experience as a great travel anecdote they simply cannot wait to regale their friends with."

Kitteh and his team jogged out of sight over a dune. I sighed and extended a hand, thumb pointing to the sky.

"We are not those people, Pudding. What are you doing?"

"Hitchhiking," I replied.

"Well, I hope the person who finds your sun-bleached skeleton gets a good laugh from their mates at the pub when they tell the story."

"Are you happy now?" I asked.

"I don't need to be happy, my mind is occupied."

"There's nothing here." I looked around. Hills made of sand in all directions. I wondered if we could navigate by the sun. Except it was shining so brightly, that it seemed to be coming from all directions at once.

"This way!" Drakeforth declared, and marched up a shifting slope.

My thumb and I waited in silent protest until he came back and walked off in a different direction. After several oddly elliptical orbits, Drakeforth stopped at the top of a dune and waved at me.

"If you've quite finished standing there like the centre of a gravity well, we need to go this way."

CHAPTER 13

The ruins of Errm were a sprawling deconstruction site where the broken bones of ancient buildings lay in regular lines. Though men and women scratched at the dirt with a hardware store's catalogue-worth of tools, they worked with the careful precision of archaeologists unearthing delicate fossils.

Several Murrai were dotted about the site, looking like fathers wondering what they should be doing with their kids on their one weekend a month together. We walked narrow paths lined with ropes that bordered carefully cut pits with steps going down through time. It felt like navigating a maze by walking on the top of the hedges.

At the centre of the bustling dig site, we stopped at tables laden with carefully labelled shards of pottery that suggested the ancient city had experienced an outbreak of stampeding bulls in the crockery quarter.

Around each of the tables, a hunched huddle of people armed with soft brushes delicately swept the last stubborn grains from the cracks. Drakeforth looked around for someone to verbally assault.

It took me a moment to find the right person. Some things are universal. In any organised work activity, the one you want is the fellow with the clipboard who isn't actually doing anything.

"Could you tell Professor Bombilate we are here?" I said.

"I'm sorry?" he lifted his clipboard to his chest like a shield.

"Professor Bombilate: we're his two o'clock."

"I…"

"Yes, we are late. Getting through city traffic is like herding cats. Best not to keep him waiting." I stared at the man while practicing the *katas* of Qualtagh in my head.

"You had best come with me," he said.

The man hurried to a tent that gave off the odd cooked smell of old canvas in the hot sun. Like two blue-plate specials moving from the oven to the warming drawer of a busy restaurant kitchen during the dinner rush, we followed him in.

Clipboard was a shadow in the gloom as he approached a table and whispered to a larger shadow seated behind it. Following their brief exchange, he whimpered and hurried into the light, leaving us alone with the darkness.

"What do you want?" the silhouette in the gloom asked with a woman's voice.

"We're here to see Professor Bombilate," I said, as if it weren't obvious.

"Why?" the woman asked.

"If you want to be paid for your help, you should have just said so," Drakeforth replied and stepped forward, his small note pad flicking open like a wallet.

"I don't want payment. I'm just not going to bother the professor over nothing important."

"Oh, it's no bother," Drakeforth countered.

"Last week we had a fellow come out and demand to speak to the professor about some Arthurian nonsense."

"I see," Drakeforth nodded. "I can assure you, we have no interest in Arthurian nonsense."

"That's unfortunate. From a scholarly perspective, the Arthurian philosophy has some really interesting elements."

Drakeforth gave a derisive snort, and said: "You'll find more interesting elements in a cup of seawater."

"I'm Charlotte, this is Drakeforth," I announced.

"Geddon Withitt," the woman replied.

I opened my mouth to say there was no need to be rude, when Drakeforth spoke up.

"May I enquire, Ms Withitt, if the professor is actually here?"

"Yes, you may," she nodded.

"Consider this a promissory note." Drakeforth. said, holding up a blank scrap of paper.

"Why do you want to see the professor?" Geddon asked.

"Flaming fluorescence," Drakeforth muttered. "Never mind, we will seek our own answers."

"We were asked to find him," I said, as Drakeforth tried to find the gap in the tent flap.

"Who sent you?" Geddon asked.

"If I understand the local economy correctly, then we should trade information to achieve an equitable outcome."

"You're not from around here, are you?"

"Is that important?" I held the woman's gaze, wilfully ignoring the angry muttering and canvas-slapping noises behind me.

"You tell me," the woman replied.

I pushed one hand into the bag I carried on my shoulder and drew out the paperback guidebook.

"There's nothing of value to me in that nonsense," the woman said, though her eyes flickered back to the book.

"Maybe not to you, but think what you could do with it."

She seemed to consider this, as a shadow moved within the shadows behind her.

"Drakeforth..." I whispered.

"The exit was right here..." He continued to bat at the canvas.

"You need to see this. At least, tell me if you see this." The strange woman came into view, emerging from the darkness the way yeast raises bread: slow, unstoppable, and quite spooky. Her hair floated in the gloom as if we were in a shampoo commercial.

The instant stretched to breaking point and I watched, transfixed, as the dark-haired woman leaned down and whispered in the ear of Geddon Withitt. Geddon gave a relieved sound and relaxed, her head slipping forward to her chest as the stifling heat of the tent turned icy cold.

"*Drakeforth!*" I whispered, loud enough to get his attention.

"I'm busy," he snapped back.

"I think Geddon is dead."

Drakeforth's struggle with the tent canvas ceased. He stepped past me and checked the slumped woman's neck for a pulse.

"What did you do?" he asked.

"Me?! I didn't do anything. It was that weird woman with the fantastic hair."

"There's no one else here, Pudding."

"I didn't kill her!"

"*Shhhh!*" Drakeforth waved me to silence. "We have to get out of here."

"Great idea." I walked to the canvas wall and started searching for the flap. "Who in the hegemony designed this thing?" I froze at the sudden sound of shouting from outside. "They know," I whispered.

"Don't get in a flap, Pudding," Drakeforth warned. "Things are intense enough already."

"I'm sure there is a time for puns, Drakeforth. Not now, of course. Not even in living memory, but I'm sure there is a time when they are appropriate."

Drakeforth joined me at the canvas and closed his eyes. With hands outstretched, he took a deep breath and jabbed. His fingertips slipped into the hidden edge of the tent flap. As he pulled the canvas aside, the interior flooded with the harsh glare of the afternoon sun. Drakeforth stuck his head out and jerked it back a moment later.

"How bad is it?" I whispered.

"I suggest you assume the faecal position," he said, his face pale.

"What is that? A squat?"

"There's a mob outside, and from the look of them, they are looking for someone to hold responsible for whatever it is they are angry about."

"We really need to get out of here," I said, and looked around for another exit.

"Wait…" Drakeforth found the hidden laces for the tent and trussed the cloth door shut. "That should hold them for… a few seconds."

We crossed the tent floor; avoiding the slumped corpse seated behind the table, we examined the remaining walls for openings.

"We should just go under." I crouched and tugged at the hem

of the tent. It turned out to be part of the floor, effectively trapping us in a large canvas sack.

"You can't hide in there all day, Bombilate!" an angry voice shouted from outside the tent.

"They think the professor is in here?" I asked the obvious questions and had the satisfaction of knowing the answer to something for the first time all day.

"Apparently, Pudding, there are people who know less about what is going on than we do."

"That is reassuring." I stepped back from the tent wall. It was as solid as a heavy-duty canvas sheet could be.

"You are challenging forces you cannot hope to understand!" the same angry fellow shouted from outside.

"Story of my life," I said.

"I wonder what he is talking about." Drakeforth stopped searching for an alternative exit and cocked his head to listen.

"We've told you before, Bombilate! This place is best left undisturbed!"

Drakeforth went to Geddon's table and started shuffling through the papers and pottery shards.

"Ha!" he said, and held up a gleaming knife.

"Great. Cut a slit and let's go."

Drakeforth hesitated. "When we get outside, we need a plan. We can't just go running off into the desert."

"That's exactly what we *should* do," I nodded with enthusiasm.

He thought for a moment.

"Okay."

With a quick swipe of the knife, Drakeforth slashed open the canvas wall. We slipped outside and tried to look casual.

"Drop the knife," I muttered out of the corner of my mouth.

Drakeforth did, and then kicked sand over it.

"In light of where we have just come from, I suggest we act like we have no idea what just happened."

"I can do that," I said, with no trace of a lie.

With our blank expressions firmly in place, we wandered around the perimeter of the tent and stood watching a group of highly agitated people yelling at the front of it.

"In other circumstances, that would be funny," I said after a moment.

"It would be funnier if the tent was trying to reason with them," Drakeforth said.

"We should slip away while they are otherwise occupied."

"Yes, we should." Drakeforth stepped forward, his arms raised. "Excuse me. Excuse me! I would like to know what you are so upset about!"

The mob turned with military precision and regarded us in silence for a moment. Then it erupted in a cacophony of shouting and fist-waving.

"Really? Well, that is interesting. I see. Indeed, yes, they should. What did you say to him? It's an idea, perhaps you should discuss it with the others? Yes. I understand. No, it doesn't work like that. Seriously, ask the cats. Where else would it go? I wouldn't have expected that either. I know, but what other colour would go with that?"

The crowd subsided into silence as Drakeforth seemed to not only hear, but listen and reply to each of their individual ranting concerns.

"Well, that's great." Drakeforth smiled at everyone. "I think we made a lot of progress here today. We'll regroup next week, okay? Great.

The mob dissolved into a loose amalgam of confused people looking embarrassed at being angry in public.

"Finally someone is listening," one of them said.

"Yeah, we might actually get them to stop," a comrade agreed.

"It is good to get someone in charge to pay attention," the first continued.

"Yes, terrific," Drakeforth enthused. "Now return to your homes, or places of employment, or wherever it is you hide from the utter futility of your existence."

Increasingly, surprise was becoming a thing that happened to other people. So I felt completely unfazed when the mob shrugged their collective shoulders and started to dissipate like morning dew in the few seconds after sunrise in the desert.

"Glad you got that sorted," I said. "Now we can get back to escaping the scene of a possible murder that we will definitely be blamed for."

"Odd bunch. They're members of the Knotsticks and are convinced that the digging is going to reveal something that is currently unknown."

I kicked the tyres on Drakeforth's last comment a couple of times. "Mass hysteria?" I suggested.

"The unfortunate thing about mass, Pudding, is that once they overcome their inherent inertia, the momentum can make large groups believe things the individual would never entertain. Or, to put it another way, the individual is less dense than the mob."

"Archaeologists dig things up." I waved at the tableau of digging figures laid out before us. "It's their mission statement. Their reason for getting up and going to work in the mornings. It is, I would suggest, their thing."

"Yet, there is a vocal group of locals who believe that things under the sand should remain under the sand." Drakeforth shaded his eyes and stared into the shimmering horizon.

"Did they say why?"

"Explanations vary; it's the way of mob mentality. As near as I can tell, however, the general consensus is that digging things up will mean they are discovered."

"Wow." I took off my hat and fanned myself with it. "Do you think we should tell the archaeologists? I mean, what if they discover something? It would be terrible."

"An admirable effort, Pudding. The question we should be considering is: Why do the vocals have such odd concerns?"

"Voc—? Oh, I get it."

"If I remember correctly, the middens were over there..." Drakeforth marched off in the direction of a dig site where labourers swarmed like flies.

Landfills are not the invention of modern civilisation. For the archaeologists unearthing (or, more specifically, *unsanding*) the ancient city of Errm, the city's trash heaps were the go-to spot for finding all kinds of interesting things. Here were tangible examples of the trite wisdom that one man's trash is another man's treasure. Especially after the trash has spent a thousand years under desert sand.

We watched the careful examination of the ancient rubbish recovered from the dig. It made the perfect advertisement for recycling. Mostly because the idea of anyone going through my bins hundreds of years in the future made me cringe.

"I never really think about it. What happens to the trash after it's gone in the bins, I mean," I said.

Drakeforth gave a snort. "Considering legions of city planners, council employees, waste disposal engineers, and environmentalists lie awake at night thinking of nothing else, perhaps you should?"

"It's not my fault," I snapped.

"Then why so defensive?"

"It's creepy. Personal things ending up in a landfill only be to be dug up and examined by people..."

"More than a thousand years later, Pudding."

"Embarrassment has no half-life, Drakeforth. Those moments when we wish the ground would just open up and swallow us are always there, and having them brought up again is the same as living them again."

The fascinating thing about embarrassment," Drakeforth said, actually paying attention for once, "is that it is one of the few times people actually experience time as it truly is." "How can embarrassment reveal the truth about time?" I immediately regretted asking the question. Drakeforth would give me an answer anyway. Telling people he knew things was more important to him than sharing knowledge.

"Time does not exist, at least in the passing sense. The entire scope of all things, all the Universes, all the dimensions, all the stuff. It's all happening all at once. You just perceive it as a matter of moving from event to event. Except, each event is static. Only your perception shifts."

"Ah, so perception is time." I wasn't going to let Drakeforth win this one without a fight.

"Sure. And a slice of bread is a sandwich."

"I don't find your analogy very palatable, Drakeforth."

"Run," Drakeforth said. Which, at the time, seemed like a poor attempt at avoiding acknowledging my cleverness. Then I noticed the knot of people gathering and whispering outside the tent.

"Do you think they found her?" I whispered. "Drakeforth? Wait for me!"

The new mob formed rapidly and gave chase. We fled across the narrow paths between the carefully excavated pits, men and women in hot pursuit under the desert sun.

I scrambled up a dune at the far side of the excavation and rolled down the other side. The disappointing part was realising that simply falling down didn't make it any easier to escape, and I had to climb up another dune, my feet digging deep into the imprints left by Drakeforth.

At the top of the second dune and breathing hard, I raised my hands and turned around. There was no one there to accept my surrender.

"Pudding!" Drakeforth popped up like a meerkat that had stepped on a Lego brick. "Keep going!"

"Do I have to?" The stifling heat made me sound whiney.

"No, I suppose not. You should have no issue at all explaining the circumstances of how you came to be in the presence of a woman now dead. The Pathian justice system is like a maze."

"I hope you mean that it is complicated."

"Well yes, and once you find your way through the labyrinth of courts the result is always the same."

I narrowed my eyes further against the glare that even my dark glasses couldn't eclipse. "What is the result?"

"You need to experience it for yourself. Words could not do it justice."

I glanced back the way we had come. The mob crested the ridge behind us, howling for blood. I sighed and stumbled down the dune. The acoustics at the bottom of the sandy valley were quite good, so I sighed again for dramatic effect and headed up to meet Drakeforth.

The sand avalanched around me, threatening to send me sliding into the valley for a premature burial. Drakeforth peered over the edge, and I am sure his silhouette bore an expression of extreme disappointment.

"Will you stop mucking about?" he snapped.

"Come on in, the sand is fine!" I shouted back.

Shadows fell across the dunes in a chilling pattern like long hair floating in a calm sea.

The shouts from behind me rose in pitch. The mob were waving and wavering. I squinted into the sun to see the cause of the distraction. A braided rope of hairy leather dropped in a neat circle around me and then jerked upwards. I was upside down in seconds, the cord drawing tight around my ankles. As I lifted off the ground, Drakeforth swung past, ensnared in a rope of his own. Under different circumstances, we might have made an extraordinary circus act.

"*Saucer-heels!*" Drakeforth yelled as he swung past.

"What?!" I yelled back.

"*Sosha-goes!*" Drakeforth shouted as we arced through the air.

"What the foucault are you on about?!"

Drakeforth pointed upwards.

Ohh, *sausages.*

CHAPTER 14

In the time of goats and grass, trees were already rare on the vast plains of Errm. Arthur's people, the nomadic goat herders and balloon animal artisans, spoke of The Tree. No one knew for sure The Tree existed. Legend said close to the ground, goats had stripped the bark of the trunk back to grey wood. Out of their reach, a bristling crown of thorns hung like sea mines protecting clusters of small fruit.

They said in ancient times the bite-sized fruit of the sacred tree was highly prized as a sweetener in ceremonial drinks. The acrid bark tasted so bitter most goats only tried chewing it once.

Traditionally, young and idealistic pilgrims sought out the sacred boughs of The Tree. Some made the journey for spiritual reasons, others in an attempt to impress their peers, or because they had lost a bet.

As the desert replaced the grass and the ancient nomadic culture moved to the city, The Tree faded from legend into myth, forgotten by everyone except a few scholars and people who liked to spend their weekends dressing up in historical costumes while pretending that life was much better a thousand years ago.

Every generation, the story would come around again: a campfire tale, an allegory, a parable, or a fable. The details changed with each translation. The elements were always the same: find The Tree and it will grant you the answer to any question. Wishes would be granted and the secrets of the Universe would be revealed.

That no one had ever found The Tree didn't stop people seeking it, spending their life-savings, and in some cases, paying with their lives.

CHAPTER 15

S*ausages, floating in the air.* It didn't seem possible. Yet, there they were, proving me wrong.

We gained altitude and dunes and the angry mob slipped away beneath us as we swayed gently in the shimmering air.

"Drakeforth…"

"I have no idea," he replied.

"Balloons!"

"Bless you."

"No, it's balloons. Lots of balloons, tied together. "Interesting." Drakeforth stared at the horizon.

We hung beneath a net of hundreds of sausage-shaped balloons. It would have been more impressive, if the only thing stopping us plummeting to a certain death wasn't a creaking cord of braided leather.

The blood rushed to my head until I felt sure keeping my eyes closed was all that stopped them popping out of their sockets.

"Is there someone we can talk to?" I asked.

"What about?"

"Oh, you know, the weather… The price of tea in Chandallah. Nothing important."

"And yet the weather is the most important factor of the price of tea in Chandallah. If the growing season has been too dry, the nature of the tea crop will be entirely different than if there has been higher-than-average rainfall, and this will impact the price."

"How have I lived this long without knowing that?" I wanted

to fold my arms, to really drive home how utterly unnecessary Drakeforth's explanation was. Except vertigo meant I didn't know which way to fold my arms against gravity, and I ended up smacking myself in the face. "Oww!"

I heard the zipping sound of something sliding down the leather rope, and then the strong smell of someone who probably couldn't describe the inside of a shower cabinet from memory.

Through watering eyes, I made out a blurred shape. He was naked and very hairy, or wearing clothing made from half-cured skins.

"Should we go inside?" he asked.

"You need to put us down! Right now!"

"No, after you. I insist," he said.

"Let us go, or I'll skin you alive," I smiled sweetly.

"Does anyone have a torch?"

"Down. Now." Using vocal techniques to influence outcomes is harder than you would think when you are hanging upside down.

"I suppose we have to go down. If we go up, we won't have gone anywhere." He waved his hands in the air and the rope around my ankles started to wind up.

Our captor rose beside me, chattering constantly. Most of what he was saying made no sense. I focused my attention on tracking Drakeforth, who was uncharacteristically silent as we were elevated into the belly of a sausage balloon.

Hairy hands landed me like a trophy fish on a wooden deck, and the leather rope loosened from my ankles.

Drakeforth thudded down beside me, and the skin-wearing man bounced over him and removed the bonds around his legs.

"Any chance of a cup of tea?" Drakeforth asked, sitting up.

"I'd settle for an explanation, and being returned to earth." I wiggled my toes, feeling the circulation return to my feet.

"Tea?! Tea. Tee-hee…? Tree!" The man leapt from the deck like a banned toy bursting from its box. He scrambled up a complex rigging of leather straps and disappeared into the canopy of suspended junk.

The floor and walls suspended beneath the cloud of grey balloons were as random as the crazy paving of Pathian walkways. Scraps of wood, bits of bone, animal skin and some kind of plaster created a mosaic pattern of materials and colours. While it looked strong enough, the entire structure creaked and moved in the air. I took a deep breath and tried not to think about dying.

"Drakeforth? Do you think we can climb down a rope or something?"

"I'm sure we could." Drakeforth stood and helped me up. I brushed the sand off my clothes and took stock of our situation.

After a few seconds, I concluded that I lived a life overstocked with strange circumstances and bizarre occurrences.

"But why would we?" Drakeforth added.

"Because it seems rude to impose on this…gentleman, without an invitation or any warning that we were going to drop in on him and his…flying balloon collection."

"Goat intestines," Drakeforth said, and went to examine the bindings on some of the more ramshackle parts of the cabin.

"Strong language, but okay."

"The balloons are made of goat intestines. It's an ancient nomadic tribal art form, though I can't say I have ever seen anyone take it on a tangent that would lead to a flying machine. I think it warrants further investigation."

"We already have an investigation that requires further investigation. A missing professor. Your wife—"

"Ex-wife," Drakeforth corrected.

"Not relevant for the purposes of this demonstration," I snapped.

"Why mention it, then?"

"I didn't! Eade did. When I first met her. She made a point of mentioning it."

"Why would someone build a machine like this?" Drakeforth asked.

Much like a life flashing past in the moment of death, an entire epic of adventure, romance, betrayal, and ultimately self-discovery, flashed through my mind. Instead, I sighed and said, "Why not?"

Drakeforth whirled and fixed me with a wide-eyed stare before marching across the creaking wooden deck and seizing me by the shoulders

"That," he whispered hoarsely, "is the most profound thing I have ever heard you say."

"You're welcome?"

"Yes…" Drakeforth released me and shook himself to recover. "Yes, indeed, we are both welcome. Otherwise, we wouldn't be here."

"Not exactly reassuring."

"Reassurance is for people who stay home and darn the holes in their socks." Drakeforth set his hands on his hips and peered upwards through the tangled network of creaking leather cords and gently pulsing sacks of inflated goat-gut.

"Persimmon?" Our host dropped to the deck and thrust a tomato at me.

"Uhm, no thank you. I'm fine."

"Don't mind if I do," said Drakeforth, leaning past me and taking the offering. He sniffed it and made an appreciative sound.

"I'm Drakeforth, this is Pudding," Drakeforth said.

"Persimmon?" our host asked again, another of the tomato-berry-things in his hand.

"No, thank you. I think that's a tomato."

"It's definitely a persimmon," Drakeforth replied.

"It looks like a tomato."

"You say tomato, I say persimmon."

"Persimmon?" The man with the fruit was looking at each of us in turn, his offering gesture becoming more adamant.

"Very nice," Drakeforth smiled and nodded in a way I'm sure he thought was reassuring. Our host whimpered and recoiled slightly.

"I have barely slept in the last couple of days, I'm not even sure what day it is. Drakeforth?"

"Hmm?" he said, with a mouthful of persimmon.

"What day is it?"

"Moogay," he replied.

"What's your name?" I asked, stepping between the two of them. "Charlotte," I said carefully, pointing at my chest.

"Goat," the man replied, pointing at himself.

"Yes, you are wearing what smells like dead goat. But what is your name? I'm Charlotte." I repeated the gesture.

"Goat," he waved again and nodded.

"Hello, Goat, where are you going in this flying machine?" Drakeforth asked.

Goat turned on his heel and scuttled to a battered trunk tied to one corner of the deck. The metal hinges screeched as he heaved the lid open and rummaged inside. We waited until he returned with a rolled-up scroll of well-scraped hide. With a grand gesture, he straightened and unfurled the skin. *"Tr-"* Goat stopped and turned the skin up the other way. "Tree!" he said.

A crudely painted white shape on the smooth side of the skin looked almost like a tree. Grey-white bark, gnarled branches and strange dark lines that were either leaves and twigs, or hair.

"That's a lovely picture, Goat," I said reassuringly.

Drakeforth stepped forward and snatched the scroll. Holding it up to the light, he studied it intently.

Goat's nostrils flared and his eyes went wide. "Pedestrians!" he roared.

"Drakeforth… Give the nice man back his picture."

"The Tree? You are out here looking for The Tree?"

"Tree!" Goat beamed.

"Pudding," Drakeforth announced, "this man is completely mad."

"Really? What gave it away? His unkempt appearance? His half-cured animal skin wardrobe? His strange manner?"

"He is seeking The Sacred Tree."

"Looking for a tree in the desert? Isn't that like looking for an iced tea shop out here?

"Only if people had lost their lives looking for a particular iced tea shop which no one had seen in thousands of years."

"Persimmon?" Goat asked. I took the fruit without a word.

"I thought there weren't any trees in a desert. It's part of the whole desert thing. If there are trees in it, surely it's more of a forest fire waiting to happen?"

"Goats," Drakeforth replied, rolling up the scroll and handing it back to Goat, "are hard on trees. They tend to chew the bark off them. Once a tree has had its bark chewed off all the way around the trunk, it dies. Much like if someone was to chew the skin off your neck."

"Eww," I said.

"Trees have always been mythical in this part of the world. Only the nomadic nature of the goat-herding clans gave the grass a chance to grow. Even then it took a particularly grim breed of grass to survive."

"Strain," I corrected.

"Massive strain," Drakeforth nodded. "The stress made the grass extremely tough, and probably quite fatalistic."

"Goat is out here looking for a mythical tree?"

"Pretty much. It doesn't exist, of course. It's the idea that people become obsessed with. With enough desire, ideas take on a reality of their own."

"Wishful thinking makes wishful reality?" I asked.

"All the wishing in the world won't make a tree grow," Drakeforth replied.

"I wish it did."

"Tree!" Goat whooped and leapt into the rigging again. He leaned out into the desert sun and peered into the distance, his eyes narrowed against the glare.

"The puzzle of the persimmon has been solved," Drakeforth announced.

"Oh, good. I was beside myself with worry about the persimmon puzzle." Tiredness and a general sense of being buffeted by events beyond my control had honed my sarcasm to a sharp tone.

"Up here," Drakeforth said. I sighed and went to see what the fuss was about.

CHAPTER 16

The sight of Drakeforth's feet suggested he had climbed a few rungs up the network of leather rigging. I sighed again and climbed up beside him. On the flat roof of the cabin, closer to the gently undulating gas-filled sausages, a small orchard of smaller trees had borne fruit. In an equally constrained enclosure beyond the trees, a tribe of goats watched us with intense interest.

"Hey, Drakeforth. You look like you have seen a goat," I said with a grin.

"Indeed, and the source of our host's persimmons." Drakeforth climbed up onto the farm deck, and against my better judgement, I followed him.

The trees were waist height, growing closely together and rooted in rich, dark soil.

"Drakeforth," I said carefully. "Are there large areas of Pathia were fertile soils are common place?"

"No," Drakeforth replied, and bent to examine the tree crop.

"So, if you were going to grow fruit trees and goats, what would you do for dirt?"

"It depends entirely on where you were going to live," Drakeforth replied, moving on to examine the goats.

I stepped carefully around the garden box and frowned at the goats.

"Sand can make an excellent building material, if you combine it with something binding and make bricks out of it."

"Something binding?" I wanted to hear him say it.

"Yes, a high-fibre diet is essential for adding bindy-ness."

"And the fruit?" I grinned.

"Goats can eat it. Gives you plenty of essential nutrients, and if you overdo the binding, fruit can be very persuasive."

"You should be an advertising copywriter for laxative products," I said.

"Advertising is all lies, told to people who want them to be true."

"Ah, so advertising is the same as religion?" I turned the persimmon over in my hand and tried to remember if I knew how to eat the strange fruit.

"Not at all. Advertising is telling lies to people who want them to be true. Religion is telling lies to people who know them to be true."

"Hang on, how can religious people know something is true and at the same time, they know it to be untrue?"

"Faith, Pudding."

"Sure, but you are the living embodiment of the god Arthur, are you not?"

"I'm more sharing my personal space with a god. I am Vole Drakeforth, who has the living spirit of Arthur co-habitating in his consciousness."

"Okay, so you are a god. Or a person containing a god. Kind of like one of those containers you put leftovers in."

"Make your point, Pudding."

"Then you know that religion is real. At least, Arthurianism."

"Of course religion is real. It's a very specific construct with a foundation in some universal truths." Drakeforth seemed to be waiting for me to reach a conclusion that he had arrived at an hour ago.

"And yet, you have just said that religion is not true."

"I also said that faith is how truth and untruth become interchangeable."

"It doesn't make it right though." I was running out of road for this argument and had a nagging feeling that I had missed my exit. Whatever conclusion Drakeforth was expecting us to rendezvous at, he was probably on his second cup of tea by now.

"Sure it does. People are made up of a multitude of simple

systems, and that leads to complex behaviour. Accepting things on faith is the least surprising outcome." Drakeforth shrugged.

"I've heard you rail against religion often," I reminded him.

"Religion, certainly. It's a manufactured system of idiocy. Remember, Pudding, people like to believe in things. It gives them comfort."

"No one would ever believe half the things I know to be true." I ripped the persimmon open and wished I had a spoon.

"Exactly." Drakeforth patted a goat that was trying to eat his trousers.

I ate my persimmon without using a spoon.

CHAPTER 17

G oat made tea as I watched in morbid fascination. Surely, at some point he was going to laugh, tell us it was a joke, pull out a proper kettle, some nice Oolongjera, and make a proper cuppa.

Instead, he beamed proudly and added a blend of dried persimmon leaves and sand packed into an old sock. Instead of water, he used goat's milk. He heated the milk by adjusting a mirror that caught the sun's rays and focused them to a point of light that seared the wooden table. From the black lines that crisscrossed the floor, tabletop and walls, it seemed it was something he'd practised often.

The golden dot of light touched the open pot of milk, which started to steam immediately. After a few seconds, Goat jerked the mirror away, breaking the beam as he dunked the sock into the hot milk.

"Water would be fine..." I whispered hoarsely.

"Noooo, it really wouldn't," Drakeforth murmured.

With a ceremonial gesture, Goat lifted the sock and then dunked it once, twice, and a third time. The dark liquid seeping through the fabric did look like tea.

Goat dealt out small earthenware bowls as if they were playing cards. Shaking his hands out, he took a deep breath and lifted the sock out of the pot with the care and focus of a bomb disposal technician with hay fever.

Taking a pair of bone sticks in his other hand, he used them to squeeze every drop out of the bulging sock, and laid it aside.

With both hands, he lifted the pot and filled three of the bowls.

Drakeforth and I accepted the offered cups. I was watching Drakeforth out of the corner of my eye, waiting to see if he would drink it. He bowed his head and then tilted the cup, taking a small sip. Drakeforth set the bowl down, nodded and gave a grim smile.

"A proper Pathian tea ceremony. Quite the honour, Pudding."

"Indeed it is," I smiled and nodded at our host.

"Drink your tea, Pudding." Drakeforth was still holding his set expression. Goat was beaming at us both, the expectation clear on his face.

"I hate you, Drakeforth," I murmured, and sipped the strange potion. "Hey, this isn't bad," I said a moment later. The taste was unlike any tea I had drunk before. It was refreshing, complex, and hardly tasted like goat-smell at all.

"Tea-hee-hee!" Goat toasted us with his own bowl and took a long sip. I took a second mouthful and discreetly rescued a goat hair from my tongue.

"The time has come," Drakeforth said, "to speak of many things. I'd like to start with your search for the tree."

"Tree," Goat nodded, and saluted us with his cup.

"Tree!" I agreed and took another swallow.

"How long have you been searching for The Tree?" Drakeforth asked.

"Tree!" Goat toasted me again and I echoed him, as a wonderful warmth flowed from my stomach and through my tired bones, before blooming in my head like flowers in a time-lapse video.

"Drakeforth, this stuff is great," I said gravely.

"It is the fermented goat's milk that adds that special something," Drakeforth agreed.

"Very special," I nodded.

"Goat, how long have you been searching for The Tree?" Drakeforth asked again.

Goat scratched the matted lump of hair that had once been his beard. "Tuesday," he said eventually.

"Tuesday?" Drakeforth asked. "You've been looking for The Tree since Tuesday?"

"Tuesday?" Goat asked.

"Yes, you said you have been looking for The mythical Tree since Tuesday."

"Tuesday..." Goat took another sip of his tea.

I was delighted to discover that if I held the cup just so, and blew bubbles, the resulting foam tickled my nose.

"Why are you looking?" Drakeforth asked.

I elbowed him, keen to share my discovery. "I made bubbles," I said.

"Yes, you did. Goat, what started you on this search for The Tree?"

"Tree!" Goat leapt up from the table and ran to the battered trunk. He returned with the skin-scroll and unfurled it again to show us.

"Tree!" I shouted, saluting with my cup.

Drakeforth stood and marched over to Goat. Taking the scroll, he tossed it aside and shook the ragged man by the shoulders.

"I need you to focus. Tell me what you know."

I got up and had the disconcerting feeling that my head was rising at half the speed as the rest of my body.

"Steady...on," I muttered. It was as much of an instruction to myself as it was to Drakeforth. The pattern of fractured light coming through the holes and gaps in Goat's airship cabin whirled like a kaleidoscope.

"We also die..." I whispered. The vortex of colours echoing that fateful moment in Godden's office.

I fell to my knees, everything colliding and spinning, falling into darkness. Like a rock in the tempest, the discarded scroll did not move. Focusing on it helped my nausea, and I stared harder as I crawled over to it.

The image of The Tree appeared painted on the scroll. Like one of those weird pictures that change from a rabbit to a goldfish the more you look at it, the patterns shifted. Layers of grey-white ink cracked and lifted. Dying butterflies of ash peeled away from the scroll and took flight before melting like dark snow.

Veins of empathic energy pulsed through the scroll, searing the carefully sketched roots and branches. It all became very clear in that moment, and I felt unexpected relief at how neatly everything fell into place.

"Tree…" I whispered, a slack and drooling grin spreading across my face.

CHAPTER 18

"Pudding?"

Warm air wafted over my face, and I frowned at it.

"Pudding, wake up."

"Don't want to," I mumbled.

"I quite understand. Now wakey-wakey!"

My eyes opened, while my face arranged itself into a frown.

"I don't feel well," I announced to Drakeforth as he helped me up.

"No one does," Drakeforth said, patting me on the shoulder.

Goat sprang into my personal space and peered closely with an expression of exaggerated concern.

"Tree?" he asked.

"Yes," I replied after a moment. "Yes. I understand about the tree."

Goat's eyes searched my face. I worked on smiling reassuringly, and felt like I was leering. I shook myself.

"Right, well, I'm fine. How are you?"

"Fine," Drakeforth agreed. "Goat? All okay?"

The strange man shrugged as if not entirely sure.

"Wait. He put something in the tea. He drugged me!"

Drakeforth went to the abandoned table and examined the cups. He sniffed each one in turn, wiping a finger through the remnants and tasting it.

"Goat milk tea," he declared. "Rather good, but completely normal."

"Well, he gave me *something*," I insisted.

"Goat?" Drakeforth asked. "Care to explain?"

"Huge," Goat replied. "Huge whispers. No one listens to shouts. Shhh!" He cocked his head and nodded. "Erskine. Uncouth." Goat nodded again, as if agreeing with someone we couldn't hear. "In-dubby-tibbly?" he asked. "In-doo-dub-it-ably?" Goat's nose wrinkled in distaste. "Gab, gab, gab." He made an apologetic gesture at us, as if he were on a phone call and the person on the other end didn't have the decency to get to the point.

I stared at the man curiously.

"Drakeforth, do you have any experience with people hearing voi—?" I caught myself asking one of the daftest questions ever conceived.

"Why yes, Pudding. I have experience with people hearing voices. I am also knowledgeable about people seeing colours, I have a nodding acquaintance with people feeling confused and I even find reports of people believing things to be plausible."

Ignoring Drakeforth got easier with practice.

"Is it possible that he is using some kind of earpiece? A communications device both small, and highly advanced?"

"Indubitably," Drakeforth said.

"Oh, don't you start." I stepped close to Goat and snapped my fingers until he blinked and fixed his attention on me.

"Pay attention. Real person talking here. Okay? Good. Now, what did you put in my tea?"

"Oolong, fresh milk, two-thousand years of cultural tradition and pageantry… Oh, and essence of persimmon rind."

"You may have just had a funny turn in the heat," Drakeforth suggested.

"Fainting would be a funny turn; I saw…" I shuffled a mental deck of word cards looking for something to describe it. "I saw some really weird things. Clearly, this man spiked my drink!"

"Spike?" Goat asked. "Spike no milk. Spike," Goat put his hands on his head and curled his fingers.

"What in the Cretaceous is he talking about?"

"I think he is saying that Spike is a buck, a male goat," Drakeforth replied.

"Why are you so calm? This man tried to drug me!"

"Pudding, there's no evidence of that. You are overreacting. Besides, even if he had, I wouldn't let any harm come to you."

I made angry fish noises until my astonished fury subsided enough for me to speak.

"That is very kind of you, Drakeforth. However, what in the half-eaten sandwich makes you think that protecting me from some kind of assault is more important than say, people not committing assault in the first place?!"

Drakeforth frowned, then started to speak, thought better of it and went back to frowning.

"Charlotte," he announced. "You make a very good point. I apologise. Goat, we need an explanation."

"And another thing," I interjected. "Just because you have apologised to me for the first time in living memory, does not make any of this okay!"

"Tree?" Goat squeaked. "She see Tree?"

"Yes, I saw something that may have been somewhat tree-like."

Goat nodded and scrambled to retrieve the tree scroll. "Tree!" he jabbed at it.

"Maybe it's déjà vu, but I am sure I have seen that before," I muttered darkly.

"Déjà vu is actually—" Drakeforth started. I shut him up with a glare.

"Not the time, Drakeforth. I saw this, and there was empathic energy. Double-e flux. The driving force of the modern world, all over it. And it went beyond the scroll. It went, well, everywhere. In lines."

"You saw lines of empathic energy?" Drakeforth asked, going for the silver medal in the *stupid questions* Olympics.

"Yes. It was very disconcerting. However, I know what I saw: Double-e flux. It's everywhere. At least, it's everywhere according to the scroll." I stopped and took a deep breath; confusing myself was exhausting.

Drakeforth took the scroll and held it up to the fractal pattern of sunlight that ricocheted through the gaps in the cabin of Goat's airship.

"It's Living Oak," Drakeforth announced.

"It's all Living Oak," I corrected. "You probably know all this, but allow me to explain, because I need to hear it to make sure I'm not completely ninth-hole bunkers."

"Go on, then," Drakeforth said.

"Living Oak, the original source of empathic energy. Discovered by my great-grandfather and developed by his cronies into one of the greatest examples of things we would rather not think about in the history of everything. Which is all the exposition I have breath for right now. It now seems that every fragment of Living Oak is connected to every other fragment. This scroll is made from the bark of a Living Oak. It's connected to every other tree and log and even my desk. Goat's magic tree is also Living Oak. Why that makes it important to find it, I have no idea. Perhaps he had a bad breakup and has been out here sulking for so long that he's been consumed with guilt and can't find the right way to go back and apologise."

Drakeforth remained silent.

"And here's Vole with the weather," I said.

"You're mostly right," he said. "I mean, I can't speak for Goat's guilt, or his relationship status, though I imagine if he's been away for this long, it is likely that ship has sailed into a burning bridge by now."

"That's sad," I said.

"Indeed. A tragedy. Speaking of relationships. This is going to be bigger than Living Oak. It *is* the relationships."

"Which relationships?" I felt like I was trying to grab the thread of a conversation during a high wind.

"The Relationships," Drakeforth said with a tone that made proper nouns raise their collective eyebrows.

"Oh right, why didn't you just say so?"

"Everything exists because of its relationship with everything else."

I nodded, "My pending migraine exists entirely because of my relationship with you? I can believe that."

"Exactly. However, not the point I am trying to make. How would you describe the size of the Universe?"

"Uhh… Big?"

Drakeforth shook his head, "The Universe isn't big. It's every-thing. It's all there is. You can't think of the Universe as being defined by ends or edges. Why do you think cats like to climb into boxes?"

I hesitated. Obvious reasons for this cat behaviour immediat-ely came to mind. They like to be closely confined? It lets them hide from predators? They are hinting they would like to be sent by first class post to somewhere with better food?

"No," Drakeforth said, even though I hadn't answered his question. "Cats have perception beyond human comprehension. Not only can they see at night, they perceive the subtle clockwork of the Universe. Every probability, every sub-atomic particle, every entanglement. Being cats, of course, they ignore most of this until it forms something they might like to eat. Cats sit in boxes because it gives the Universe limits. It lets them feel *this is the dimension of my Universe. Everything else is outside of it.*"

"Interesting idea. Though, the box is part of their Universe, which means of course, the box has no limits."

"Exactly." Drakeforth looked like he wanted to seize my hand and shake it vigorously for understanding his point. He quickly regained his composure. "It is the relationship between the cat and the box that defines the Universe."

"I seem to remember a point being made about the connection between all Living Oak?" I asked. My headache rose like a spring tide on the beach of my frontal lobe.

"Living Oak is entangled. Every particle is infused with the same energy as the whole. Every tree is part of a singular mass. If you take one sliver of Living Oak from a tree, it will still hold the same empathic energy as the entire tree. Though it will have a far smaller presence."

"Which helps us how?" I asked.

"Clearly, if we have a parchment made from the bark of Living Oak, then we have a connection to the Living Oak that it came from. Not only that, but we have a connection to every other tree and piece of Living Oak."

"So, if the tree that Goat is so desperate to find is also Living Oak, then we can find it, because it is all connected..."

"Yes," Drakeforth said.

I sighed. "Next time, maybe just explain using bullet points? Perhaps a simple infographic?"

"You cannot distil understanding of the Universe into something so simple," Drakeforth replied.

"Cats manage it," I said.

CHAPTER 19

I woke up feeling light-headed and overly warm. The sun was close to the horizon; I hoped it was sunrise tomorrow and not sunset today. Sleeping was difficult enough without messing up the timing of it.

The hammock I lay in was a comfortable net of goat-leather strips. I wriggled slightly, getting the sling to swing and watching the way the red and orange dapple of sunlight rippled through the cracks and gaps in the cabin.

Moments of complete peace are rare, so I gave this one my complete attention. I could go back to sleep. Really get some rest. Sleep until it was all over, let someone else do the work and wake up to read about it in the papers. Like everyone else, I would be concerned about it for half an hour until the next news story took over the collective consciousness of the world.

Goat emerged, shuffling with the dim-witted semi-consciousness of the freshly woken. He paused in an errant beam of sunlight, scratching himself before stretching mightily and yawning. He turned, arms raised above his head, and we made eye contact.

A moment passed during which I kept my gaze locked on his face.

"*Meep!*" Goat yelped, and scrambled up the rigging towards the orchard.

"Morning, Pudding," Drakeforth announced with unusual cheer.

"Good," I replied and swung the pendulum of the hammock until I reached escape velocity and landed on my feet.

"A near perfect dismount," Drakeforth said.

"It is morning isn't it? I slept through the night?"

"Yes. Tea?" Drakeforth raised a chipped mug with a faded cartoon character on it.

"Not after last time," I frowned.

"Regular tea. A blend of some rather stale Oolong and a sprinkle of Ashma."

"Thank you."

"There would have been more Ashma, but it was mouldy."

"You had me at regular tea."

Drakeforth handed me the cup; the tea was hot and refreshing. I drank it and tried not to think about watering persimmons. "Do you think Goat has a toilet?" I asked.

Goat's bathroom had seen less water than most Pathian plumbing. He had emerged fully dressed by the time I returned and we let Drakeforth do the talking as we occupied ourselves with not looking at each other.

"I have been going through your charts and…notes," Drakeforth said. He lifted a pile of screwed-up scraps of paper on to the table. "The good news is that you have been to many places that may have been the site of The Tree, but actually aren't. At least, they weren't when you went there."

"Tree?" Goat asked, and gnawed on a strip of goat jerky.

Drakeforth peeled a crumpled egg of paper. "There is a theory that The Tree has quantum properties. This makes actually finding the drumming thing almost impossible."

"What quantum properties?" I asked.

"Like any decent sub-atomic particle, we can either know where the Tree is or how fast it is travelling."

"Oh, that quantum property," I said. "Are you sure that is why no one has ever found it? Don't things have to be, well, sub-atomic to have quantum properties?"

"Of course," Drakeforth said. "What no one considers is that if you bring enough sub-atomic particles together they can make up quite a large piece of reality."

"All of it, I should think," I said.

"Precisely. The trick is bringing all that quantum potential with you. Living Oak manages that up to a scale of one tree."

Drakeforth rarely spoke with such passion about anything he wasn't angry about. I finished my tea and sniffed a piece of goat jerky before putting it back on the plate.

"How do we find The Tree, if we can only know where it has been?" I asked.

"Or how fast it is travelling," Drakeforth replied.

"Either way, it makes finding it impossible."

"There is a way." Drakeforth collected Goat's bark manuscript and unrolled it across the breakfast table. "You are tuned into the channels of interconnected empathic energy."

"Okay."

"So we use you to confirm The Tree's current position and its momentum."

"Have you considered that maybe The Tree doesn't want to be found?"

"That will be the second question we can ask it," Drakeforth said.

"The first being...?"

"The whereabouts of Professor Bombilate, of course."

I almost asked who Professor Bombilate was, and then I remembered and felt guilty about the lapse.

"Of course. We should get started then."

"Goat!" Drakeforth barked. Goat flailed wildly and fell back off his stool.

"Raise the mainsail, weigh the anchor, bilge the pumps! We have places to go and trees to see!"

"Tree!" Goat yelled from the floor, a fist pumping the air in triumph before he rolled to his feet. Goat leapt into the rigging and then slid down a rope to the cabin deck. We watched as he threw himself around the flying ship. Tugging on goat-hide straps, turning wooden pegs and pulling on levers. The ship continued to meander through the air at the same sedate pace.

"Well..." I said after a few minutes of watching a distant sand dune keeping its distance. "This is exciting."

"Do you feel anything?" Drakeforth asked.

"Too much, too often," I replied. "It's exhausting."

"Specifically, are you feeling any empathic energy flows in a particular direction, either converging on or coming from the tree that Goat is obsessed with finding?"

I took a deep breath. On the exhale, my breath misted as if I was somewhere cold. It also sparkled as if I was in a blizzard of glitter.

"Pudding?" Drakeforth's voice came from a great distance. I blinked, my eyelids crashing down with the weight and gravity of neutron stars.

"Yes…" I whispered down a tunnel of swirling light. The warm glow of empathic energy sparked in a living network that pulsed with an infinity of synchronised heartbeats.

"It's kinda cool," I murmured. My words sparkled, sending glowing snowflakes of energy spinning into each other, where they burst into shards.

"Follow the energy to its source," Drakeforth said.

Empathic energy funnelled into a whirlpool that stretched to infinity. I let my consciousness tip forward and I plunged into the vortex. As everything accelerated, the blur of my velocity knitted the sparks together with faint lines that I told myself were light.

A constellation took shape as I plummeted down the seemingly endless tunnel. Like people who see the face of Arthur in their burnt toast, I comprehended the shapes by making them familiar. "I wondered where you got to."

The woman with dark hair smiled at me in that mysterious way that no one really can.

"You're everywhere," I said. "You show up and interfere, or stop me doing something, and then you disappear again. I have no idea if you are trying to ruin my life or save it. Your only redeeming quality is that you don't have Drakeforth's sarcasm."

The woman raised a pale, glowing finger to her cold, sparkling lips and silently shushed me as I crashed through her face. Her image shattered into stars, and the stars broke.

In a place of moving light, refracted, reflected, imprismed, and scattered, I found The Tree.

"No wonder no one has ever found you," I said to The Tree. "You probably don't exist."

Energy coursed in lines from all directions. It flowed up the trunk to spread among the endless branches and leaves, spilling out into everything in countless streams.

"Not the source, a conduit," I said. "Energy is neither created nor destroyed, just endlessly cycling."

I could have stayed there forever. I may have already. Rising from the stream of consciousness only required me to open my eyes.

"What did you find?" Drakeforth asked.

"You don't know?"

"Pudding, I'm not Pathian-trading with you. There is too much at stake."

"Arthur doesn't know something?" I was amused but unsurprised.

"Arthur knows all. So humour us by telling me what you found."

"The Tree. It's not what you think. There is no plant growing in some hidden desert oasis. The Tree is everywhere. Connected to everything."

"Now you understand," Drakeforth said.

"Yes, though I don't think you do."

"I find it better not to," Drakeforth replied.

I cleared my mind with a sigh. "You could have told me that before!" I punched Drakeforth in the arm.

"I find it is better to learn things at your own pace," Drakeforth said. "That way, you can make your own mistakes."

"And learn from them," I replied.

"Mostly it stops you blaming anyone else."

"How does this help Goat? Or us, for that matter?"

"You found the answer when you went, wherever it was you disappeared to."

I frowned, "Uhm, no I'm quite sure I said I didn't find The Tree."

"You found it. You just don't know where it is going," Drakeforth said.

"Because we can either know where it is, or where it is going?"

"We know where it is going," Drakeforth replied.

I thought for a moment. "Everywhere...?"

CHAPTER 20

"Would it help if we rowed?" I asked after several dull hours of gentle drifting across the endless sand of the Pathian desert.

"It might," Drakeforth replied from under his hat. He had retired to his hammock while Goat steered the airship towards the horizon.

My internal dialogue went round in circles. *Where are we going? Oh, but if we know that, we won't know how fast we are travelling.* I could see how fast we were travelling. I could shimmy down a rope, run a few laps around the shadow of the airship, and casually climb back up before it had travelled more than two ship-lengths across the burning sand.

With Drakeforth hiding under his hat, I was left to stare out at the drifting dunes. The worst part of being on such a slow boat was how it left me with no one to interrogate except myself.

All right, Pudding. We're going to get to the bottom of this.

Yes, I mentally nodded. *We're already scraping the bottom of the barrel, so why not make a go of it?*

Well there's no need for that kind of attitude.

Are you sure?

Winning an argument with my inner voice was unlikely. It felt easier to take action instead of talking about it.

"Goat!" I shouted.

"See!?" he bellowed from the helm with such intensity, we may as well have been in the grips of a terrible typhoon and not drifting through the calm air as sedately as lint.

"You don't know where we are going!" According to Berkeley Upsqueak, if you are going to subvert a question by making it a statement, then speak with confidence and volume.

"What?!" Goat reacted as I had hoped.

"You have no clue where we are!" I enunciated each yelled syllable.

"I don't?"

I took a deep breath. Berkeley had also said that if you find yourself going through homophones, then keep going.

"No idea!"

I waited for the weight of my words to have the desired effect. It took a moment, and then the ship groaned as the air had intensified. I grabbed the rail and hung on. Overhead, the tight mass of inflated goat intestines squeaked indignantly under the strain of the rising wind.

The tones and shades of the sky changed so rapidly it felt like one of those interior design paint books had been riffled through at close range. The swelling clouds went from *Snow Cake* to *Crusty Frypan,*and my skin tingled with the building static charge of impending lightning.

There is no way this is going to work, I warned myself.

"Shutup," I replied aloud.

Everything went from mildly off-putting to extremely weird in what might have been a few seconds. I sighed and closed my eyes.

Cats arranged themselves like self-cleaning gargoyles along the convoluted ledges and edges of the Pathian Museum of History. The building itself was a low hill of stone blocks and pillars that gave the impression it had been built by a legion of blind stone masons, each of whom had no idea that anyone else was working on the project.

Goat's ship appeared in the shadow of this eye-twisting edifice with a sound similar to a cat coughing up a fur ball.

Space and time, and all the possibilities between, hurriedly got their story straight and the sky returned to normal. Except for the floating mass of inflated goat intestines with the haphazard wooden cabin swinging underneath.

"We've arrived?" Drakeforth asked, joining me on the deck.

"Yeah," I nodded. "It wasn't that difficult, once I realised we can't possibly know where The Tree is, or where it is going at the same time."

"Which means the chances of it actually being here are as remote as Nin's hot-chip caravan in Yambake, Malakam," Drakeforth replied.

"Is that remote?"

"Stupidly remote." Drakeforth adjusted his hat. "Come, Pudding, we have a library to explore and possibly rob."

CHAPTER 21

With Goat's help, we dismounted and trod the warm sands towards the museum. I followed Drakeforth on to a narrow flight of stairs that went up at an angle as if it were climbing a hill. The stairs switchbacked across the front of the building and we covered more ground than necessary in reaching the grand entrance.

To my complete lack of surprise, the massive doors were made of stone. Drakeforth pulled a rope handle protruding from the centre of one. The metre-thick slab of rock swung outwards with the silent ease of a whale doing a headstand.

We walked into an interior that had a pleasant chill to it, as if the only cold air in the country had been safely stored here.

I inhaled the special smell of museums: the slightly dusty, oddly chemical, musty scent of old things gathered in one place. It smelled like curiosity and the thrill of discovery.

My pace quickened, along with my pulse, as we entered the museum gift shop. Arrayed on shelves and racks were souvenirs and T-shirts with catchy slogans. Everything about the place felt as tacky as a mile of spilled honey. She was here already, sitting cross-legged on the counter top, chin in her hands watching us come in. Her impossibly dark hair stirred gently, like eggs in a soufflé mix.

Drakeforth moved left with the certainty of a bloodhound suffering a sinus infection, and collided with a postcard stand.

"Where is everyone?" I whispered.

"I'm here, you're here," Drakeforth replied.

"And everyone else?" I chose to ignore his wilful ignorance of my hallucination, who was now lying on her back on the counter, one leg crossed over the other knee, wiggling her toes to the beat of some unheard music.

"Minding their own business, I expect," Drakeforth said.

"Do we pay an entry fee?" I asked.

Drakeforth stepped around a display of icecube-sized stone blocks, labelled as genuine pyramid stone. "In Pathia, this place is the equivalent of a bank. Getting in is free; getting out, however, may cost you everything."

We passed through an archway of perfectly stacked stone blocks, flanked by a pair of murrai. After my experience with the Godden Corporation's answer to humanity, these animated stone statues made me nervous.

"Do you think these are real?" I whispered.

"No, they're an illusion; it's all done with mirrors and clever use of light."

"I mean: are they actual murrais?"

Drakeforth gave them a moment of his attention, reaching out and tapping one on its chiselled features. "Yes."

"They remind me of those RABITs the Godden Corp was making."

"Similar idea, though these are artisanal pieces. Carved from local stone by masters of the art."

"I thought the Pathians didn't use empathic energy?"

"They don't, at least not anymore. They did use it, centuries ago. When the pyramids were built and the murrai were empathically powered. Then attitudes changed, the murrai fell out of favour and became museum pieces."

"What about the ones we saw carrying litters?"

"It's not like they break down, some people still use them. It's just harder to make a living when you are competing for work against a stone man who doesn't need payment or bathroom breaks."

"I didn't read any of that in the guidebook."

"Tourism is also an illusion, Pudding."

"Wait..." the thought that had been itching at the back of my mind for a while intensified. "Godden and his fellow deplorables discovered Double-e flux a century ago. How can that be, if the Pathians were using it hundreds of years ago?"

Drakeforth rolled his neck as if my insistence on finding out things caused him pain.

"There is a school of philosophy that suggests if you can't see something, it doesn't exist. This makes as much sense as most philosophy, in that it's good for a laugh, but really is best not given too much attention when it comes to practical applications like manufacturing products for the visually impaired. There is also a raft of other disciplines that explore the cycle of the rise and fall of civilisations, the acquirement and loss of technology and, oddly enough, the constant of tea."

My nodding along stopped. "The constant of tea?"

"Every civilisation throughout recorded history, and probably before, has had a form of tea. It has the same social structures and is always prepared using the same basic ingredients of hot water and dried leaves of a local plant. Tea is the one constant found in all countries, cultures, and civilisations. People have gone centuries without cottoning on to the idea of the wheel, or the prepaid gift card, but every single one of those tribes, regardless of size or complexity, has understood tea."

"Which relates to my original question how, exactly?"

"It's called *tangential speech*, Pudding. I thought you studied language structure at university."

I shrugged, my mind flashing to a joke the linguistics lecturer told about a man who fell asleep while sunbathing naked.

"Empathic energy was known to, and utilised by, the ancient Pathians. They stopped using it centuries ago and since then, like most countries separated from others by an ocean, Pathia remained happily isolated and doing its own thing. Exactly why Pathians stopped using empathic energy has always been the subject of conjecture. Now, I suspect it was because they realised what it actually is," Drakeforth continued.

"They figured out that empathic energy is the life energy of actual people?" I asked.

"Enough to make the decision to stop using it for anything,"

Drakeforth replied. "The knowledge appears to have fallen out of use for centuries, then rediscovered by three college students with questionable morals."

"How can the murrai keep functioning? They should need refuelling, or something."

"No one is certain. They just keep working."

"Energy cannot be created or destroyed, just transformed. So the murrai are self-contained batteries of double-e flux of some kind? Surely, someone has taken one apart and seen how they tick?"

"That's the thing." Drakeforth waggled his eyebrows in a mysterious way. "It has been done, there's nothing inside a murrai except more murrai. Stone, all the way through. Regular desert rock. There is no reason they should be moving at all."

"Maybe they keep going because they don't know they shouldn't?"

"Quite possible," Drakeforth nodded. "Best not tell them then."

Beyond the archway, a sign welcomed us to Exhibit Hall A. The hall was filled with well-lit glass cases. I stopped at the first one, which held swords. The display card explained that they were actually part of an ancient Pathian ploughing machine.

"Pathians have always been a practical people," Drakeforth observed. "They invented farming implements for use in activities both agrarian and aggressive, depending on the season."

"I remember Dad saying that blood and bone was good for the garden."

"If that were true, Pathia should be a botanist's paradise."

You are a tourist, I reminded myself. *So do something touristy.* The museum was laden with exotic and interesting artefacts. I investigated a glass cabinet with a display of coins. Various historical attempts at currency. Tiny fragments of order. The stamped profiles of various kings, queens, emperors, chairpersons, and the occasional elected official, decorated the back of each token.

I moved slowly through the gallery, intrigued and absorbed by the long tapestry of history so carefully preserved here. Given that Pathia now operated on some kind of knowledge-based economy, I wondered where the important information was. This was fascinating, but farming implements, old coins, and decorated shards of pottery hardly seemed to be the secrets of an entire nation.

A large metal cylinder stood against one wall. It seemed oddly out of place with *Do Not Touch* tape criss-crossing the surface. Scraps of packaging material and tools were stacked up next to the gleaming metal object. I wondered if it was an historical relic or part of the air conditioning.

I stopped and frowned. Hushed voices, speaking with intense anger, came to me from among the shelves and haphazard stacks of innumerable artefacts.

"Will you keep your voice down?" a man insisted.

"No, I won't. In fact, I think I will raise my voice. How do you like them guppy-apples?" It took me a moment to recognise Eade Notschnott. She sounded angrier than a football full of hornets.

With Drakeforth having disappeared into the silent chambers of history, I was in the awkward position of interrupting what appeared to be a private argument. Or possibly a crime of passion with no witnesses and plenty of time to come up with a plausible alibi.

"What in the name of Saint Capricious do you expect me to do about it?" The man had taken to sounding petulant.

"Careful, you know the penalty for invoking such names," Eade warned.

"If I go down, you go down. They'll bury us head first next to each other."

"In the same plot? Well that would be appropriate, I suppose," Eade sounded more relaxed now. Her opponent was defeated and the rest of the argument was just the cuddling afterwards.

"I can't give you anything," the man insisted. "It's all monitored closely. You could end more than your own career if you insist on making this outrageous claim public."

"You won't be held accountable. It has to have happened without your knowledge," Eade soothed.

"Without my knowledge?!" the man snapped, and then got control of himself. "Without my knowledge? Nothing could happen to that collection without my knowledge. I'm the curator. I'm supposed to be the one with *all* the knowledge."

"Oh come on," said Eade balancing exasperation with charm. "If you knew everything, you would have retired to the Aardvarks or Glystonberry by now. Cashed up and free."

"Knowledge never lets you be free," the man replied. He sighed. "If you can find out who is responsible, then we can fix this before anyone else finds out."

Eade gave a snort. "Who is going to find out? No one cares."

"I care," the man insisted, the tone making it clear that his wounded pride was breathing its last.

"Of course you care, as do I. And whoever committed this grave crime must have cared, too."

"We cannot let anyone find out," the man insisted.

"We also have to investigate. We cannot let them get away with it."

"They have already gotten away with it!" the curator snapped.

"Only if we let them," Eade replied.

"Pudding?" Drakeforth called from the dark wings of the Hall of Histrionics, where displays of ancient theatrical costumes and props were kept.

The two disembodied voices stopped immediately and Eade came bustling out of the rows of shelves.

"Charlotte?" she blinked.

"Hi," I said, with a guilty wave.

"What are you doing here?" Eade asked.

"It's a museum. I'm a tourist on vacation. It seemed like the logical place to visit."

Eade nodded, her cold stare suggesting she didn't believe a word I said.

The curator had slipped away into the archived shadows.

"Pudding, I found something." Drakeforth joined us and almost reared back when he saw Eade standing next to me.

"Eade," he said, making it sound like a bad word.

"Vole," she smiled.

"What are you doing here?" they both said at once.

They locked eyes in silence. I waited until the silence went beyond palatable to kneadable. With a dusting of flour and a spoonful of fresh yeast, it could have been bread.

"I was just saying to Eade, that visiting the museum seemed like the perfect activity while we are on vacation."

"We're not on vacation." Drakeforth's eyes never wavered from Eade's line of sight.

"Of course we are." I tried to keep things light by smiling. The rotten ice of embarrassment was starting to give way and threatening to plunge me into a chasm of anxiety.

"You're not on vacation," Eade echoed. "I know why you are here. We may as well get this over with." She blinked, a gesture as sharp and subtle as a paper cut.

We followed Eade past rows of stone shelves. Each was stacked with scrolls, books, and cartons. She came to a round vault door, shining steel and matt gold, glinting in the gloom. I felt a pang of homesickness for my own vault as Eade peered into the retina-scanning sensor. She spun the spoked wheel and with a final glance around, she pulled the door open.

CHAPTER 22

Moosebumps rippled up my arms as soon as the door closed behind us. Unlike most of Pathia, this room felt cold. Not icy cold, just dry and chilled. A wine critic might say the room had pear and chamomile notes, with a light bergamot spice in the finish.

The walls were familiar stone with no obvious mortar, or grout, or…?

"Drakeforth, what is holding this building up?" I asked, a weird form of claustrophobia suddenly pressing in from all sides.

"Faith," Drakeforth replied immediately.

"Really?" I raised a cynical eyebrow.

"Of course not. The entire building is the product of millennia of trial and error in the fine art of stone masonry, engineering, mathematics, and architecture. Not to mention the applied science of interior decorating."

"Interior decorating is hardly an applied science." I almost snorted, not willing to be caught out twice by sarcasm.

"Clearly you have never studied the delicate interplay of balance and harmony in a matrix of repetition on a sub-basement scale."

"Well no, but—"

"Over here," Eade announced, "is a stela by Stella." She waved at a worn panel of carefully etched sandstone. "It depicts Arudda, son of Attila, sister of Asail, famous for her navel manoeuvres."

"A seafaring family?" I asked.

"Asail was a renowned belly-dancer," Eade replied. My brain

would go cross-eyed before I could be sure that she wasn't being sarcastic.

"Moving on," Eade said. "We now come to where the trouble started."

Drakeforth trotted on her heels like a trained weasel. I lagged behind and took a moment to appreciate the familiar oddness all around me.

My mother had taken a fine arts degree and turned it into a career restoring artefacts in museums. They are special places, full of fascinating history, culture, and T-shirt slogans. Like a movie set or a stage, what you see is just a façade. The presented displays and props are carefully curated images. An illusion for public consumption. The work that goes on behind the scenes is where the magic truly happens. People like my mother studied, archived, protected, and curated everything from A'zron rings to gourds of Z'aron. Most of the things in museums remain unseen. Which, if you have seen a Z'aron gourd, is not such a bad thing.

The room reminded me of the few times Mum had taken me into her workplace. None of the polish and romance of display choreography found in the museum out front. This was all steel shelves and lighting as far removed from romantic as a garland of fish-guts.

On a steel table with work lamps that would not be out of place in an operating theatre, lay a large slab of stone. I stopped and peered at it. Chiselled words in an ancient script formed neat lines and the occasional stick figure. Someone had been working on translation and I read a note stuck to one carefully cleaned section.

Translation GS of Murk. Quanta VII. Section B. Linear Apex.

The student came unto the Master meditating in The Garden. Under The [Living Oak?] *Tree. And spake he unto Him.*

Master. What is the most annoying question in the world?

The Master replied: Good book?

And the student was enlightened.

"Charlotte," Eade called. I straightened with a guilty start and joined the librarian and Drakeforth at a polished stone bench. A wooden case, about the length and width of an extraordinarily tragic coffin, waited for us. The wood showed signs of exposure to the elements. The roughly hewn panels were cracked and dried to a silver-grey. A strangely familiar scent of herbal oil wafted from the interior.

"Patchouli!" I said.

"Bless you," Eade replied. "Vole, put the gloves on. Take that end, and help me open this."

Drakeforth's scowl deepened and he slid his hands into some soft white gloves. With a sulky air, he helped remove the lid of the case. I waited to see what could be in such an ancient box in the depths of a back room of Pathia's most secure containment facility.

"I see," Drakeforth said, his scowl deepening.

"I don't," I spoke up, trying to lean forward to change that.

With Eade giving instructions, they lifted a bundle of grey fabric out of the box and set it down on the bench. Under the bright lights, the sheet had the same aged silver look as the wooden case. Eade delicately unfolded it, revealing a faded pattern of lines, circles and stick figures that appeared to be drawn with mud.

"Behold, the Shroud of Tureen," Eade announced.

The annoying part of my subconscious sighed as I wracked my brain trying to think why I should know what the Shroud of Tureen was.

"It's a dirty sheet," Drakeforth said. He worked the linen gloves off and dropped them on the table.

"It sure is," Eade said, with sickly sarcasm. "*The Moaning Lizard* is just a bit of paint slapped on a canvas, too."

I clenched my fists to avoid high-fiving Eade for her casual takedown. Drakeforth gave her a mildly suffering sigh.

"Eade, the Shroud of Tureen is a joke. It's what happens when a good idea gets written down and is subsequently pillaged by idiots who wouldn't know the truth if it convinced them to marry it so it could get a work visa to Pathia."

"Oh, Drakeforth." Eade almost looked concerned. "You're letting your issues show."

"My issues!?" Drakeforth stopped and exhaled slowly. "My issues? You lied to me. You lied to everyone. You, Eade Notschnott, are a liar."

"So?" Eade shrugged. I waited for Drakeforth to explode. To rant, to curse and stamp his foot. To let his outrage erupt like a volcano and seal us all in the scalding ashes of his fury.

"Nothing, I was just making conversation." Drakeforth was as calm as a corpse. I found it more unsettling than his outburst.

"Fine," Eade replied, making it clear that things were so far from fine, you would need a valid passport to get anywhere near fine.

"I remember seeing a sen-show about the Shroud of Tureen," I spoke up. "It's the controversial Arthurian artefact, kept by those guys… the uhm…Fossicks?"

Never being one to miss an opportunity to make someone feel inferior, Eade spoke up. "The Knotstick Order. Also known as *The Men of The Cloth*."

Drakeforth picked up where she drew breath. "Those waggamoles have been claiming that the shroud is the original text of Arthur's first attempt at recording his teachings."

"Well, you would know, right?" I asked.

"Of course. And while yes, there was a sheet used to record my original ideas, this is not that sheet."

"Scientific analysis," Eade insisted with extra emphasis, "has proven inconclusive on the origins and provenance of the shroud."

"It's a sheet. It could have come from any shop that sells bedroom linen. It has faded marks of dirt on it. There's no mystery, no divine value to any of it. It's just mud."

Eade put her hands on the edge of the table and leaned in. "Vole, there have been centuries of warfare, persecution, peace and enlightenment because of the ideas recorded on that ancient fabric. It has no value, because it is priceless."

Drakeforth's eyes narrowed. "It's only priceless because hapless fools are still paying for it with their lives and with their reason. I should have kept the ideas to myself and never tried to explain them."

"You're talking nonsense, Vole," Eade straightened.

"Nonsense is a social disease. Any two people come into contact and sooner or later, one of them will convince the other of some nonsense. In the worst cases they combine it with their own nonsense, and it mutates into some abomination of a new idea that is complete and otter nonsense."

"Yes, he does mean *otter*," I interjected, before Eade could.

"The Shroud of Tureen is the greatest artefact in all of Pathia. In this or any other library," Eade insisted.

"It's a soiled piece of linen. There is more spirituality in a mocktail," Drakeforth snapped.

"The belief of the faithful is what gives it spirituality," Eade replied calmly. "Of course it is a sheet. It is *the* sheet. Did Abomasum of Biddlebunk not say *'sheet happens'?"*

Drakeforth waved the claim aside. "Abomasum may have been the second Grand Linteum of the Knotstick Order, but he was the first to realise that the public interest in the Shroud could have a commercial value. It's the only reason the order still exists."

"The Knotstick Order are one of our most favourable patrons. Without their knowledge, we couldn't afford to keep this place open."

"It isn't really, though is it?" I suggested.

Eade blinked for the first time in a while and cocked her head in my direction. It was the view a worm would have right before the bird strikes.

"Isn't what?" she asked.

"Open. I mean, look around you. There's no one here. It's the weekend, assuming you have weekends in Pathia. So the doors should be open. Tourists should be gawping. Bored kids should be slouching around the exhibits. Tour guides should be droning on. Except there's no one here."

"This is the premiere repository of knowledge in all of Pathia. We can't let people just go wandering around. What if they learned something?"

"Imagine," I said.

"The entire economy would collapse. There would be rioting in the streets. Information would become…" Eade trailed off in shock.

"Free?" Drakeforth suggested.

"Biscuits and tea!" Eade yelped. "That would be even worse!"

"I get it," I said soothingly. "Pathia runs on a knowledge economy. It's weird, but it works for you. How does anyone learn anything?"

"Through hard work and fair payment, obviously," Eade replied.

"International trade must be a nightmare," I said.

"I'm sure it is no worse for us than it is for anyone else." Eade folded her arms in a defensive posture. "And you are still talking nonsense, Vole."

"Am I? Fine. I'll let Arthur convince you." Drakeforth closed his eyes and started to mutter under his breath. *"Yes now. No, this is not the time to arg—All right. Yes, I have been keeping a tight rein on things. Look, will you please ju—"*

Drakeforth's eyes flicked open and I felt a chill. Vole Drakeforth wasn't in right now, but we could probably leave a message.

"The Knotstick Church," Arthur said in a voice like warm charcoal, "are just one of a legion of people who completely missed the point. Arthurianism has always been about the incredible nature of what we think of as the Universe. It was never about answers, or understanding why things are the way they are. It is about the pleasure of wonder. The sheer delight of realising the fundamental truth of how the Universe is *really, really, weird.* Making it into a religion completely ruined it. Sure, they have contributed to the advancement of theoretical physics and that has made for some pretty neat inventions and technology. But at what price?"

"Empathic energy," I said. "The faithful giving up their quanta to provide the power to make the world run. That is the price."

"Chimp change," Arthur said. "The quantum effects of Living Oak would have been discovered and used for profit by someone sooner or later."

"Possibly, except that under the guise of Arthurianism, the Godden Corporation got away with murder for decades."

Arthur shrugged Drakeforth's shoulders. "The Godden Corporation killed a few people, it's nothing personnel."

"You mean, nothing personal," Eade replied.

"Nothing *personnel*. They used their RABITS as assassins. No animals were harmed in the harming of the enemies of Godden."

"Well, we are talking about a dirty sheet," I reminded the conversation.

"It's more of a dirty secret," Drakeforth replied in his usual voice. It seemed that Arthur had hung up on us. "This—" he jerked a thumb at the cloth "—is not the Shroud of Tureen, it is a fake."

I waited for Eade to retort; instead, she shrugged and then looked at me. "What? He's not wrong."

CHAPTER 23

"How long has The Shroud been missing?" Drakeforth asked.

"Since Professor Bombilate disappeared," Eade said.

"Could he have taken it with him?" I asked.

"Yes, perhaps he thought it needed cleaning," Eade said, with acid in her tone.

"And how long has he been missing?" I asked. Surely at least one of us could act like an adult.

"That would depend on your perception of time," Drakeforth interrupted.

"No," I said firmly. "It wouldn't."

"A couple of weeks," Eade said.

"Have the authorities been informed?" I could hear myself asking reasonable questions like a proper adult. I wondered how long I could keep it going.

"Yes," Eade replied.

"And?"

"They said that Professor Bombilate was quite capable of making his own decisions and maybe I should give him his space."

"Really?" my left eyebrow sprang into its customary position of surprise.

"Of course not. They gave me a form to complete and said they would look into it."

"And did they?"

Eade gave me a concerned look. "Charlotte, are all our conversations going to be this tedious?"

"Uhm, no? Forget I mentioned it…" I mumbled.

Drakeforth cleared his throat. "The authorities, in any situation, will do as little as possible. Not, I would add, due to any lack of will on their part. It's usually something like budget cuts, or resources, or an impossible caseload."

"Wait," I said, seizing the opportunity to interrupt. "How do you know the perils of police work?"

"I've had my share of involvement with the lawn."

"You obfuscated your way out of a traffic ticket!"

Drakeforth snorted. "Only because if they had investigated further, certain allegations and cases that remain technically open, would have added to the complexity of the situation. In short, once accused of murder and technically not acquitted, one tends to avoid the lawn."

"What?" I managed.

"Technically open," Drakeforth repeated.

"You make it sound like you got off on a technicality," I frowned.

"Yes, let's say that's what happened." Drakeforth nodded with enthusiasm. "We have more pressing matters. Specifically, a fraudulent sheet and a missing informist."

"Well…we could ask his friends and family where he might have gone."

"Did Bombilate have friends and family?" Drakeforth asked.

"I never asked," Eade shrugged.

"You worked with the man," Drakeforth reminded her.

"I couldn't pick my colleagues' friends and families out of a police line-up," I said.

"Exactly. I worked with Professor Bombilate. I didn't have to get to know him to do that."

"You could have been married to him," Drakeforth muttered.

"We could start with where he lived?" Keeping these two on track was harder than herding cotton balls in a wind tunnel.

"Why not?" Eade smiled coldly at Drakeforth. "I'll check the records office for his home address." Eade walked stiffly out of the room, leaving Drakeforth and myself in a chilled silence.

"Would you tell me if you had murdered someone?" I asked

"Probably," Drakeforth replied. His attention focused on folding the Shroud and returning it to its box.

"You didn't mention that you were married," I continued.

"It was annulled." Drakeforth raised his head and thought for a moment. "At least, I think it was annulled."

"You're not sure?" I felt an unpleasant sense of familiarity.

"Well, I did have Eade declared legally dead. It seemed cheaper than hiring a hitman to do it for real."

"Drakeforth, you can't go around having people declared legally dead. Especially when they're not actually dead."

"Makes you think." Drakeforth closed the lid on the shroud. "If you are legally dead, and are in fact still alive, are you living illegally?"

"It would depend on what you were doing while alive," I replied. "For example, if you were committing murder, then yes, you would definitely be living illegally."

"I didn't murder anyone," Drakeforth announced gravely.

"Oh, good."

A crash of glass and splintering of wood broke the silence. We looked towards the hanging weight of the round vault door we had passed through. Out there, the museum waited, empty and still. Except for a rhythmic thudding, that came closer with each thud.

"School group?" I ventured.

"I usually slip away at this point," Drakeforth said, casting about for an alternative exit.

"It does avoid awkward questions. What about Eade?"

"I'm sure she will be fine and if I'm wrong, then she will have more pressing concerns than being abandoned by us."

With a scream of metal, the vault door was wrenched off its hinges and tossed into the room.

"Skating skeletons!" Drakeforth cried. We ran for the back of the room. A wall stood as a silent reminder that there was no escape that way.

A murrai ducked through the open doorway. Its massive stone shoulders caught on the steel frame and ripped it out as easily as walking through a spider web.

"Is it malfunctioning!?" I yelled as the walking statue stood up and straightened.

"It shouldn't be functioning at all!" Drakeforth yelled back.

I ran around the edge of the room, dodging around tables and trying to avoid the lumbering statue that stomped further into the room. The murrai swung an articulated arm and a fist, larger than my head, cracked the stone floor.

"Follow me!" I yelled, and ran for the only exit. I high-stepped over the rubble and glanced back. Drakeforth was not as close behind as I'd expected.

"What are you doing?"

"The Shroud is the key to all of this. Forged or not. We can't leave it behind."

The murrai's head snapped towards Drakeforth as he flipped the lid off the wooden box.

"Look out!" I grabbed a throwable chunk of masonry and proved it. My missile bounced off the murrai's back with all the devastating impact of a butterfly's boop.

Drakeforth had the folded cloth under his arm. He jumped aside as the murrai smashed the wooden case and the table with a single blow.

The machine studied the remnants for a second while Drakeforth ran to meet me.

"Why did you stop?" he gasped.

"Oh, you know. I wanted to see what would happen."

"Thud, splat, most likely," Drakeforth replied. "Oh look, it's worked out that the shroud isn't there anymore."

The murrai had finished tossing the fragments and had worked its way through the long arc until it faced us again.

We ran through an exhibition hall and skidded into a hard-right turn. I took the lead and raced towards the archway that would take us to the gift shop and exit.

Drakeforth grabbed my arm. "Two!"

"Three!" I replied automatically, and lunged forward.

"There were two murrai," Drakeforth reminded me. I recoiled from the archway as if it was the stage door to an open mic night.

"What are the chances of both of them coming to life and being homicidal?"

"It's probably just a coincidence," Drakeforth suggested and took a careful step towards the archway between the merchandise and us.

"A case of mistaken identity," I nodded, almost tiptoeing.

"There will be an investigation, of course."

"A lengthy report will be written," I replied.

"Public apologies will be issued."

"Media statements, carefully worded to express regret."

"Without actually accepting responsibility," Drakeforth said. He flatted against the wall of the arch and peeped into the foyer beyond.

"Okay, its clea—" Drakeforth scrambled backwards as the second murrai rammed through the wall in a cloud of dust and refrigerator magnets. "Belay that!"

"Just what I was thinking!" Squeezing between two display cabinets with my back pressed against the nearest wall, I tried to appear like an exhibit.

Drakeforth danced around looking for somewhere to hide. The murrai plodded forward, its stone head grinding as it followed him.

I squealed and ran towards the ruins of the gift shop when the murrai stomped past. "Drakeforth, come on!"

Drakeforth stepped to the right, and the murrai mirrored his movement. He hopped left, and the murrai followed him again.

"You dance divinely," Drakeforth told it. "But I am afraid I must be going now." He ducked under a swinging arm and bolted into the foyer.

"What the Hibernian is going on!?" Eade emerged from behind a non-descript office door.

"Murrai. Attempting to redecorate," Drakeforth replied. The noise of the two stone men trying to turn around in the confined space sounded like they were blocking each other worse than the rocks that built this place.

"Vole, what did you do?" Eade folded her arms and glared.

"I didn't do anything!" Drakeforth affected a shocked expression.

Eade rolled her eyes. "Of course you did. You're just too conceited to recognise whatever it was."

"We should go, before someone turns up and blames us for the mess," I said.

Eade hesitated, and then nodded. "Fine. Out the front door."

CHAPTER 24

Outside, night, much like half of Exhibit Hall A, had fallen.

"Do you have a car?" I asked Eade.

"I normally call a litter, using the phone inside."

"A spare pair of sandshoes?" Drakeforth asked.

"Oh, for figurine's sake. We should start walking." Eade marched down the ziggurat-zag of the narrow switchback stairs towards the world's most monotonous beach.

"Which way did Goat go?" I asked Drakeforth, as we followed Eade towards the sand.

"Considering the prevailing winds, that way I should think."

"He can't have gone far."

Drakeforth scanned the night sky. "A lesser man would be embarrassed by the shortcomings of his chosen form of transport."

"You're not embarrassed?" I'd spoken before I could congratulate myself on my wit.

"What? Oh yes, you should hashtag that one."

The grand entrance of the museum was no match for the combined momentum of a tonne of animated stone. The murrai ignored the stairs and slid down the balustrade that formed a decorative rail between the slab steps. Cats scattered and then regrouped to watch the proceedings from a better vantage point.

"Well, that escalated quickly," Drakeforth announced. We ran faster. The murrai executed a graceful dismount and landed in synch up to their hips in the sand. We used the moment while they pulled themselves out of the soft grains to increase our lead.

A long, rolling, and entirely unacceptable sound bubbled through the air.

"Really, Drakeforth? You could say 'excuse me'."

"It wasn't me," Drakeforth replied. The wind passed again and a shadow blocked the stars.

The murrai clambered up the dune, arms outstretched and their carved expressions stony as we scrambled up the knotted leather ladder and onto the deck of Goat's airship.

CHAPTER 25

"We were supposed to find The Tree," I groaned.

"The tree that can't be found?" Drakeforth muttered from the deck to my right.

"Yeah."

"Not finding it is just as important as finding it."

I sat up. "We found Goat and the map by not looking for them. We found the museum by not looking for it."

"It's the Trouble Theory," Eade said. She had found my hammock and was excavating a persimmon with a spoon as she rocked gently in time with the ship's motion. "I won't bore you with the math. Basically it states that the likelihood of finding trouble has a measurable value that is inverse to the amount of energy expended avoiding trouble."

"And yet if you go looking for trouble, you are bound to find it," I said.

Drakeforth stood up and brushed himself off. "She's making it up, Pudding. It's an attempt to make her sound more educated."

Eade shrugged and tossed the husk of her freshly excavated persimmon over the side. Goat yelped and ran across the deck, tying a knotted cord of leather around his waist as he went. We watched as he dived over the rail and vanished.

"We should probably see if the fall killed him," Drakeforth said after a few seconds.

I plucked at the taut cord. It twanged with a deep note that went down the scale until the rope creaked. With a grunt of effort, Goat climbed over the rail.

"Persimmon," he panted. He carefully set the rind aside and unhitched the rope.

"Are you okay?" I moved closer to Goat until the smell of him stopped me.

"Do they validate parking?" Goat asked.

"I'm glad you're okay and the persimmon was rescued." I smiled and nodded, a blush rising on my cheeks. Why was I embarrassed? I wasn't the crazy one. Was I?

"Drakeforth, care for a recap?"

"It's certainly the time of night for it," Drakeforth agreed.

"Eade, if you could try your absolute hardest to stay quiet until I have finished, that would be appreciated," I said, before she could finish drawing breath.

"Professor Bombilate. Informist and archaeologist, is missing. The Knotstick Order think he was on to something at the dig in Errm. They also have a vested interest in the Shroud of Tureen, which we have discovered is a forgery. Eade, in her position as librarian at the Museum, was aware that the Shroud was fake. Someone else knows about the Shroud too. I heard Eade arguing with the curator of the museum. They were concerned about their secret being revealed. Shortly afterwards, we were attacked by two murrai. Which, according to my Pathian guidebook, are not known for attacking people. All this after we escaped not one but three angry mobs, yes Drakeforth, I include the entire motorist population back home in that number. We met Goat, who is on a quest for a mythological tree. The only way we can find it, is to not look for it. We didn't find it, because it is all around us. Empathic energy. Everything is connected. The Tree is Living Oak, and Living Oak is empathic energy condensed, just like everything else. Except, I don't know, vibrating at a different frequency?" I ran out of things to say. No one laughed, so I waited a few seconds. Still nothing.

"Well that's it. I mean, everything that I can think of right now."

Drakeforth pushed his hat back on his head. "Succinct. Wouldn't fit on a T-shirt. But not bad for a recap."

"The story so far. Who cares? We know what has happened.

It's what happens next that I want to know about," Eade said from her—*my* hammock.

"Right, I mean we all do. Except, how do we know what happens next?" I looked around, half expecting a sign to point from the sky to the answer. Maybe a flashing light.

"We should have a cup of tea," Drakeforth said. "Pudding, can you find somewhere safe to store this?" He handed me the folded Shroud.

"Tea, excellent, I'll help." Eade flipped easily out of the hammock.

"Great. Tea. Yes. I'll give it some more thought, while you make tea." I held the fake Shroud of Tureen in my arms as they walked away. I tried to ignore that I could really use a cup of tea right now. I needed to find a solution. Then to celebrate with a cup of tea.

It was tempting to climb into the hammock, wrap myself up in the ancient sheet, and hope that fate would take care of things while I slept through the next decade.

Fate is a nice excuse. It wraps things up in a sweet-roll of fatalism. Nothing we do has any impact on what is already going to happen. The really smug answer to any challenge is that we have no way of knowing what destiny or fate hold for us. Destiny, of course is simply fate in sweats and no makeup, jogging with us on the journey towards the inevitable.

The inevitable journey, I thought. Well, we're never going to get where we are going at this speed. A murrai could walk fas—. I stopped that train of thought with the emergency brake of panic. Racing to the side of the deck, I peered over. Nothing but empty sand going about its business of making silicon valleys and dunes. Regretting my burst of adrenaline-fuelled enthusiasm, I tucked the grey sheet into a shelf, then ran to the other side and looked down. This area of desert was so similar to the other side they could have been mirror images of each other. Jogging and ducking under the complex macramé of Goat's rigging, I headed to the rear of the ship. There they were: stone faces turned up to us, massive feet working as sandshoes as they strode purposefully along in time with the slow meandering of Goat's skyship.

Fatalism has two children: Futility and Fatality. They are what fills the void when Hope bails.

I waved at the two murrai. "Hello!"

In perfect synchronicity, they each raised a stone arm and waved slowly in reply.

CHAPTER 26

Murrai are empathically empowered. No one uses empathic energy in Pathia anymore, I reminded myself. Except for the occasional litter service. Where do they get their empathic energy? If the murrai don't need refuelling, then their owners would be cleaning up in the business sense.

"Uhh… If you can understand me, touch your nose," I instructed. Neither murrai did anything other than continuing to plod and stare up at me. "Voice command isn't it, then," I murmured. With an exaggerated gesture, I touched my nose with a fingertip. Going cross-eyed trying to see past my elbow, I saw the murrai repeat the gesture.

"Physical gestures. Well of course, you are machines. You know, it would be so much easier if there was a control panel or a keyboard, or something that could be used to transmit instructions to you!" I had started waving my arms in frustration. It was embarrassing seeing the two murrai mimic the gesture.

"Fine." I marched back through the ship. The deck gave me the sense it had been constructed by throwing a pile of scrap wood and leather into a heap and then hammering it all together.

Coils of braided leather rope lay piled in various places. None of them seemed essential, so I took one and waited to see if Goat would voice any concern from his position behind the wheel.

The murrai were still keeping pace with the ship. I explained what I was doing as I prepared the rope. I tied a loop at each end. Then, I tossed each end at the feet of the stone men. They kept walking. The rope dragged through the sand ahead of them. The mid-point of the rope I kept for my demonstration. Lifting it up, I looped it around myself. The murrai followed suit. Now I had two murrai on the end of a rope.

Line of sight seemed to be important, so I climbed around the outside of the rigging—hardly a challenge, as the airship had more places to put your hands than a glove shop.

The murrai dutifully followed, like two massive dogs on a leash. Goat glanced sideways at me as I worked my way past. I waved at him with a free hand and saw the two stone men wave in response. Goat took a second, more careful look. His grip on reality seemed tenuous at the best of times. I hoped he would assume I was just another hallucination and dismiss my odd behaviour out of hand.

I reached the pointy end of the ship. This end had a name, like the back end. Not the same name, of course, and given how this craft had never seen water, the semantics of sea terminology seemed uncalled-for.

"Whagh!" I yelled, and almost fell off the railing. The woman with the enviable black hair was sitting at the end of the ship. Not seeing her for a while had let me think she might have been a hallucination that Goat would laugh cynically about.

I flailed, arms waving in a desperate attempt to regain my balance. She stretched like a cat and casually extended one perfectly pale hand, catching me as I tipped over the edge. Her grip was cold, and it brought me onto the right side of the rail without apparent effort.

"Thanks," I gasped. Sweeping my own hair out of my face, I blinked. She had vanished again. Unwrapping myself from the cord, I looped it around a protruding bit of wood. The two murrai had caught up with me and were now walking slightly ahead of the ship. I pulled the slack in and tied it off.

The ship twitched and followed the two murrai. Where they were going was up to them. Maybe they were wandering as aimlessly as the rest of us.

"Okay," I announced. "I know you can't understand me, but I have a talent when it comes to empathically empowered devices. Which I think includes you. If it doesn't, I'm sorry for the inconvenience. And now I'm babbling." I stopped, took a deep breath and exhaled slowly. The murrai were still striding along. We crested the ridge of a dune and started down the other side.

The murrai made better time than the desert breeze. I watched them walk and tried not to feel guilty.

"Goat!" I called from the pointy end of the ship. "Where are we heading, do you think?"

"Have you tried turning it off and turning it on again?" Goat hollered back.

There is a suggestion that some people who don't fit in are in fact geniuses operating on some entire other level. It is not clear if they are geniuses on that plane of perception as well.

If this idea had merit, then Goat might be trying to tell me something. If only I had the smarts to work it out.

"Drakeforth, do you know where we are going?"

"We are going to sit in the moonlight and drink this hot cuppa," Drakeforth replied. "Less ceremony, more spice," he added, and handed me a steaming mug.

CHAPTER 27

By the time we had gone two rounds of tea, night had become dawn, and was getting itself ready for the day. Eade had returned to the hammock and was pointedly ignoring us.

Goat approached, started to say something and then frowned, turning and listening to some hidden conversation. I waited with polite interest, mostly feigned, for him to get back to us.

In the middle of his fugue, Goat wandered off muttering, "Left, right, left, left, right. Wait, was that right, left, left, right? Who's right? My left? Where did you go?"

"We should get him some help," I said.

"With what?" Drakeforth asked.

"Working that out should be the first thing we get him some help with," I agreed, and put my empty cup down with a pang of disappointment.

"The murrai are taking us to Semita," Eade announced, driving home how seriously she was ignoring us.

"How can you tell?" I asked.

"The angle of the sun—"

I felt an irritated moment of being impressed. Navigating by the sun was the kind of amazing skill Eade would have.

"—shines through the holes in this bug-bucket of a vessel, and illuminates the screen on my mobile phone. Which is equipped with a navigation app," Eade continued.

"Annoying, isn't she?" Drakeforth's grin showed all his teeth.

"No, she's fine. Really."

"Good idea, getting the murrai on a leash," Drakeforth said.

"Thanks."

"It's that kind of lateral thinking that indicates a clear sense of direction."

"It just came to me; one of those ideas that might be just crazy enough to work."

"And yet, not crazy enough to make your friends and family concerned for your mental health."

"Speaking of concerns for my mental health, I saw her again."

Drakeforth nodded, still smiling and giving no indication he had heard a word I said.

"It seems like the sort of thing I should mention, to a friend. Casually, I mean. Something like, 'I appear to be having the oddest hallucinations'."

"Quite right," Drakeforth replied, and patted me on the shoulder before pushing past and heading to the front of the ship.

"Great. Thanks!" I called after him. "That was really not helpful at all…" I added quietly. The woman with black hair nodded with an expression of genuine sympathy.

CHAPTER 28

The outskirts of Semita appeared to float above the drifting dunes. My guidebook patiently explained that this was because the outer buildings rested atop stone pillars. The sand flowed around them, like the tide around the pilings of a pier.

The murrai turned Goat's sausage ship and skirted the city. People stopped and stared at us as we drifted past.

"Where are they going?" I asked. "We want to go there!" I waved at the city. A few gaping locals gingerly returned my wave.

"Don't tell me, tell *them*," Drakeforth replied.

"Hey! Murrai! Turn that way!" I made semaphore waving gestures and strode across the deck in the right direction. The two stone men ignored me and kept marching. Traffic came to a standstill as we sailed over a four-lane highway. Motorists seemed unfussed by two murrai crossing in front of them. Like giant whelks migrating, it was safer to give way to the unstoppable force.

The famous pyramids of Pathia shimmered in the desert sun and the murrai bore down on them at a steady pace.

"Why are we going *there*?!" I yelled at the stone men. They ignored me, which I expected. I wasn't yelling at them because I wanted a response. It was more a general outburst of frustration at the Universe.

Drakeforth appeared, sipping tea and watching our progress with the curious introspection of the casual observer.

"I should have put reins on them. Some kind of harness for

steering the dashpot things!" My frustration was still on the rolling boil.

"You appear to have stumbled on another reason murrai are no longer used extensively as a labour force for anything," Drakeforth commented.

"I feel like I tripped and fell flat on my face. How can they be so, well, useless?"

"They are articulated stone machines. They almost look like people. So we start to relate to them like people."

"Oh, they remind me of people all right. Only people could be so perfectly annoying."

"There was a time when violent crime against murrai was so common they became endangered. Many of them were destroyed by people who found interacting with the machines to be incredibly frustrating."

"I can see why. I've had computer users with more sense than these things."

"Of course you have. A toddler has more brainpower than every murrai ever created. Just because a thing looks like it should be intelligent, doesn't mean it is."

My anger faded. Frustration was exhausting and in this heat, it could kill me. I took Drakeforth's mug and finished his tea. "I feel sorry for them. They're just hammers on legs. You don't expect a hammer to follow instructions. Even if they are empathically powered."

"The idea of empowering hand tools with double-e flux was considered. There was an experiment in the early days which concluded the lack of productivity from such tools after being infused with empathic energy was only because they were inherently lazy."

"Someone actually did that?" I regarded Drakeforth with suspicion.

"Yes and as a result the development of power tools took on a new urgency."

"Did the ancient Pathian's have power tools?"

"Of course not. They had murrai."

We watched the trudging figures in silence until they reached the shadow of the pyramids of Pathia. Luckily, it was still mid-morning. If we had arrived at noon, they might have never found it.

CHAPTER 29

We floated next to one of the pyramids of Pathia while Eade and I sat in the shade of a thousand goat-intestine balloons and she offered unsolicited opinions.

"It seems obvious," Eade explained in a tone that made it clear that while it was obvious to her, she had no doubt the rest of us were completely clueless. Which made my brain clench, because she was right.

"You seem quite confident about that," I said.

"Completely confident," Eade replied.

"So explain it to me, then. Right now."

Eade actually looked up from her phone. "You wouldn't understand."

"Try me." The Pylian Juncture I got in to that phrase would have elicited an audible gasp from Bowmont the appliance salesman.

Eade sat up and put her phone away. "Well, it's the connection of things. The sum-total of the Universe. It means we're all just fumbling around in the dark. Nothing matters. This conversation. Your romantic obsession with Vole. Our mad escapade through the Pathian desert. Nothing has any purpose."

"Wait… *My romantic obsession with Drakeforth?*" A thought dawned with the full spectrum of sunlight and harmonised chorus of birdsong never seen outside of a sensie soundtrack. "You're jealous?" I blinked and said it again. "You are jealous. You are burning up because you think that Drakeforth and I are romantically involved?"

"That's ridiculous," Eade sneered, without conviction.

"Egg yeah it's ridiculous."

"Totally," Eade gave a firm nod. "Doesn't mean you're not romantically entwined, though."

"We are not romantically involved!"

"How would you know?" Eade asked.

"What kind of question is that?"

"The kind that I'm asking because you can't answer it."

"You do know I have a degree in dialectics, right?"

Eade nodded.

"Therefore answering difficult questions is what I do."

"Is that your final answer?" Eade elevated one eyebrow.

"What? No. I already said Drakeforth and I are not romantically inclined."

Eade leaned forward, her elbows hugging her knees, "Why not?"

"It's obvious. Isn't it? I mean, of course it's obvious. Isn't it?"

"You tell me." Eade seemed to be enjoying herself immensely.

"I *am* telling you. Repeatedly. There is literally nothing going on."

"Okay," Eade straightened.

"Okay," I agreed. We sat in silence for a minute. "There's just one thing."

"Oh?" Eade's other eyebrow climbed up her forehead.

"You don't believe me."

Her face exhaled and relaxed. "Of course I don't believe you."

"Well, as long as we are clear on that."

"Now, what was it you wanted to ask me?" Eade asked.

"Why did the murrai bring us here?" I repeated the question that she clearly hoped I had forgotten.

"It seems obvious," Eade started again. We were interrupted by the sound of Drakeforth's hand slapping on the rail of Goat's airship. The retired god of Arthurianism came into view as he pulled himself back on board.

"We found the entrance," he said once he stood on the deck.

"Great," Eade said, and rose to her feet.

"Why?" I asked.

"Because it was there," Drakeforth replied. "Come on, I'll show you."

CHAPTER 30

According to the guidebook, the pyramids of Pathia had no known purpose. Theories about their origin and purpose were common. Various researchers claimed they were built as temples, or tombs, or navigational guides, or as transmission beacons for some kind of interstellar radio system. What the guidebook did know is that the murrai were the primary work-force for the quarrying, transportation, and eventual placement of the thousands of blocks of stone that made up the massive structures.

At one hundred and fifty metres high, and two hundred and thirty metres along each of their four sides, the three largest pyramids were visible for miles. There were five pyramids left in the country. The rest had been demolished over the centuries to make buildings that are more practical.

We climbed down a ladder of knotted leather rope and stepped onto the sand. Drakeforth marched off immediately towards the pyramid.

I hesitated, as Goat was getting a ticket from a woman in uniform. Probably for parking his airship in a no-parking zone.

I watched as the officer moved upwind of Goat and tore a sheet off her citation pad. The information on the paper was probably worth more than the fine.

She handed it to him. Goat looked startled, accepted the offering and hugged the woman. She immediately dropped him to his knees with a swift kick and laid him out with a follow-up strike to his shoulder.

"Oh, no. We should help," I said, and hurried forward.

"Why? She's doing just fine without us," Eade called after me.

"Excuse me, officer? I'm sorry for my friend. He's not used to human contact."

Goat writhed at my feet while the woman in uniform eyed me suspiciously.

"Is this your vehicle?" She gestured at the airship floating like a conversation starter over our heads.

"This old thing? No. I'm just a passenger."

"You should know that assaulting an officer of the lore is a punishable offence."

"I can see that," I nodded, and helped Goat to his feet.

"You can pay this fine at any Lore Office in Pathia. You have twenty-one days to pay, or further action will be taken."

"Right, good. Uhm… You spelt pedestrian wrong."

"What?" the officer frowned at me.

"P-E-D-E-S-T-R-A-I-N," I spelled out.

"Pedes-train?" the officer looked at her copy of the ticket and screwed up her nose as if it smelled awful.

"Yes, from the Ancient Gherkin. *Pedes*, meaning *to clump together*, and *train*, meaning *to annoy the caviar out of everyone else trying to use the sidewalk*."

"Madam? Attempting to subvert, or otherwise disrupt the actions of an officer of the lore, in the conduction of their sworn duties, is a punishable offence."

I was in the swing of it now, so I kept going. "Officer, a spelling error in their notes would be acceptable for most people. But for someone who clearly takes as much pride in all aspects of their work as you do, such a black mark is unforgivable."

"You can accept the ticket and walk away now, or I will arrest you."

"Great idea. Okay, then." I had been smiling so widely for so long my mouth had gone dry. I backed away, dragging the whimpering Goat with me.

"All sorted?" Eade asked as she dropped to the sand beside us.

"Uh…yes," was the easiest thing to say.

"Vole is having some kind of seizure," Eade commented.

I shaded my eyes and peered into the desert glare. "Or he's waving at us and indicating we should join him on the pyramid."

"With Vole, it can be hard to tell."

We restored Goat to his feet and he trudged with us through the burning sand in silence.

No one tried to stop us climbing the block steps of the pyramid. It seemed that apart from the female police officer, we were the only ones showing any interest in the ancient structure.

"I would have expected more tourists," I said, making it look like I had stopped to observe the view, rather than trying to catch my breath halfway through the climb.

"Why?" Eade asked, and then added, "No. Don't answer that. Of course you would expect tourists. It's the off-season. Tourists are forbidden to set foot in the area of the pyramid between sunset and evening on days ending in y."

"Used correctly, sarcasm can cut like a scalpel wielded by a skilled surgeon. Slicing through the preposterous and the stupid. Revealing truth in previously unseen perfection. From you, Eade, it's more like being slowly lowered into a vat of rancid milk. Tedious and unpleasant for everyone involved." I gave her a moment to respond and then turned to see her expression. Eade and Goat were still climbing, and had left me out of earshot.

"You're right, Charlotte. I am a terrible person," I muttered, and resumed the climb.

"We were about to report you missing and send out a search party," Eade said when I reached them near the top of the pyramid.

"Sorry, I took a wrong turn, ended up on a different pyramid."

"It is easily done," Drakeforth said.

"Now about this entrance you found?" Eade asked.

"I'm waiting for the key," Drakeforth replied.

"The key?" I asked.

"She wrote me a poem. It didn't rhyme," Goat said.

"What key?" Eade asked.

"That key." Drakeforth pointed down at the ground. A freight litter was making good time across the sand, the team of bearers kicking up dust as they ran.

"It seems like a lot of people to deliver a key," I said.

"It is a lot of key," Drakeforth replied.

We watched in silence as the litter bearers came to a halt at the bottom of the pyramid. From up here they looked like grotesquely large and hideously deformed ants. They flipped a cover off the litter, revealing a carved block of stone.

The crew lifted it, and under the direction of the litter-leader, they started up the pyramid.

None of them were breathing hard when they set their burden down in front of us. It was an impressive example of human endurance, dedication to fitness training, and the effectiveness of good athletic shoe sponsorship.

Drakeforth patted his pockets and retrieved a notepad and pen. With a flourish, he scrawled something on a sheet and handed it to the team leader of Kitteh's Litter Services.

He glanced at the paper, did a double-take and then hastily tucked it into a small bag fastened around his waist.

"Thanks, man," the man said, and grinned. With a whistle and a gesture, he started the long jog down the pyramid, his fellow carriers falling into step behind him.

"While not the weirdest thing I have ever seen, it's in my top ten," Eade said.

"Top ten?" I managed to vocalise a slight sneer. "It barely registered on my *Well That's Odd,* scale."

Drakeforth swept the accumulated sand away from a depression in the carefully fitted blocks. We stood and watched in silence: it had been a long time since anyone tried to sweep the sand off a pyramid in the middle of a desert. After a minute, I could understand why.

"Can we help?" I asked.

"Do you have a vacuum cleaner with you?" Drakeforth replied, without looking up.

"No."

"Brush and dust pan? Broom? A leaf-blower?"

"No..." I hated sounding as if I was whining.

"Didn't Galfyn Ortiz make a career studying rhetorical quest-ions?"[1] Eade asked casually.

"Goat, give me a hand with this."

Drakeforth and Goat lifted the carved block. They moved it into position, wriggling the block until it grated into place with an audible clunk.

With a sound like an arthritic knee shaking something odorous off a shoe, a heavy stone panel ground open and revealed a very dark tunnel.

"Make yourselves comfortable," Goat said.

"Hang on, how did you organise all this from the airship?" I demanded.

"It's a complex plan, years in the making. Simply put, I firstly checked that the key was still under the bed at the hotel, where I had hidden it years ago. Then, when paying off the litter bearers for their previous services, I arranged for them to deliver the stone to the top of the pyramid at this time."

"You had no idea we were going to be here," I said. "So how could you know when they should bring it?"

"It was a simple deduction," Drakeforth continued. "I told Mr Kitteh at such time as the tourist creates a spectacle of rare curiosity so completely bizarre it defies the senses, gather your carriers. Retrieve the block of stone, and bring it here."

"The tourist would be you, Charlotte," Eade said.

"Clearly," I replied.

"Is it possible that Charlotte, flying past the city at the bow of an airship being towed by two murrai while barking at them like sled-dogs, triggered the delivery?" Eade continued, in the same mocking tone.

"It's possible. Should we follow them?" I walked past her and vanished into the darkness on the heels of Drakeforth and Goat.

The darkness was close and warm like wearing socks in a

---

1 In one of his many volumes on the subject, Ortiz noted: *While it is a subjective conclusion that there are no stupid questions, it is determinable through observation and analysis of verbal interactions that there are not only stupid answers. Furthermore: statistically, moronic responses make up 97% of all replies.*

sauna. With no light source, except for the reluctant glow of the outside world behind me, I walked forward with a resigned air of acceptance. The gloom parted as if it were a theatre curtain, and I stepped into a room filled with softly glowing light.

"The acoustics in here are fascinating," Drakeforth was saying. "The softest whisper can carry great weight."

"We're still in the pyramid, right?" I asked Drakeforth. Goat looked around with equal parts bemusement and nervous tic. The stone walls were bathed in a shimmering luminescence. I turned around slowly until I found the source.

"Is that...?"

"Yes," Drakeforth said.

My legs went weak and I started to sit down, only to realise that there were no seats. I slid down the wall and let my jaw sag in surprise.

CHAPTER 31

"What is that doing here?" I managed.

"A question for the ages," Drakeforth replied.

"The bathroom is upstairs," Goat said. "Make yourselves at home."

Eade lacked the sense to remain silent. "More importantly, what is it?"

"A Godden empathy engine," I whispered. "An actual engine of empathy, right here in the one nation in the world that has sworn off empathic energy for a very long time."

"Really?" Eade moved closer, "I've never seen one."

"It must be old." I tried to remember what I had learned about Godden empathy engines. "The oldest one still in use is a model seven. It runs the Python Building back home."

"How quaint," Eade replied.

"Quaint? It's not quaint. It's evil. It's confusing and worst of all it makes no sense!"

"Technically, confusion means it makes no sense." Eade's single-minded commitment to being annoying was inspiring.

"It's been a while. I'm not sure I remember how to uhh... Still, nothing like a proper Pathian tea ceremony to celebrate new... friends...?" Goat trailed off and waved half-heartedly.

I stood. This soulless corporation had always seemed determined to make my life a series of inconveniences, and the sense of frustrated fury it engendered had given me strength. "Consider what we know," I said.

"Oh joy, another recap," Eade muttered.

"This is a Godden empathy engine. A working generator using double-e flux as a power source. Which means someone is topping it up regularly. Which means someone has a use for it. Which means... Well, I don't know what it means. But I'm sure it is important."

"We could just walk out of here, close the pyramid and act like we never discovered this...thing," Eade said.

"Yes we could." Drakeforth stirred from his silent musing. "Though, walking away right now would lead to a lifetime of wondering what is really going on. That would lead to regret, and regret is a cancer for the soul."

"Drakeforth, that was both profound and somewhat bland." I regarded him with a raised eyebrow.

"Something I read on a greeting card once," Drakeforth shrugged.

I walked round the chamber. The dimensions were weird in here. I couldn't say for sure if the room was round, spherical, square, or some casual mix of the various shapes.

"Feel that?" Drakeforth asked. I nodded. I was feeling many things in that moment. I hoped that one of them was what he was referring to.

It hit me three steps later: a sudden flare of empathic energy coming up through my feet. The generator was humming away, but this felt like the entire floor had turned to lava.

"Whoa..." I swayed and held my arms out for balance.

"We're quite high up in the structure," Drakeforth continued, "which means there is a chamber beneath us of incredible proportions."

"It does?" I narrowed my eyes at the floor. "It seems solid enough."

"It does *seem* solid enough. If you were to dig down a few feet, you would agree that *seeming* is not the same as believing."

"If the Pathians haven't used empathic energy in forever, then why is all this here?" I stood as still as possible while the room pulsed around me. Closing my eyes didn't help.

"Someone has found a way to gather and store empathic energy. This generator is only using a fraction of the double-e flux stored down there."

"Which means it's intended for some other purpose?" I asked.

"Which means something that we haven't determined yet," Drakeforth corrected, and started walking around the chamber.

Eade had fallen silent, though she still lurked on the edge of my consciousness like a panic attack or a nest of angry wasps.

"Nothing to add, Eade?" I asked.

"I was just wondering what Professor Bombilate would have made of this."

"A soufflé probably," Drakeforth suggested.

"More than likely," Eade replied. "Why would someone put this…thing, in here?"

"To hide it, clearly," I snapped.

"They would have gotten away with it, too," Drakeforth said, and continued his careful pacing around the room.

"They did get away with it." I waved at the room. "Look around you."

"Medallion," Goat said, and slapped his head as if the word had been on the tip of his tongue for a while.

"It's probably just kids." A voice came from up the tunnel.

"You said that about Bombilate," a second voice said.

"Undoubtedly."

"I know that voice," I whispered. "It's the man you were arguing with at the museum."

"Erskine Uncouth," Eade whispered. She half-crouched in the realisation that there was nowhere to hide in the chamber.

"What?" I rushed to the empathy machine and determined that we couldn't fit behind it.

"Erskine Uncouth. The curator from the museum," Eade whispered.

"Indubitably," Uncouth said to his unseen companion.

"Irregardless," his companion replied. "We must get the chamber sealed again."

"That is not a word," Uncouth said.

"What are you talking about, Erskine?"

"Irregardless. It isn't a word."

"Of course it's a word. I just said it, did I not?"

"Yes, but that doesn't make it more a word than *dord*, or…or *knirf*."

"What are you babbling about?"

"I am explaining to you, my dear Nonce, that utterance does not a word make."

"Utterance? I do not utter. I speak plainly," Nonce said with an indignant tone.

"Your gums flap like fresh linen on a clothes line," Uncouth replied.

"My gums? You dare insult me? Listen carefully, Uncouth. You are a mere librarian. I-"

"I am a librarian." It was Erskine's turn to speak angrily. "But do not forget that my life has been dedicated to something very tangible. Very real. Very useable. You, on the other hand, are a purveyor of fantasy dressed as indisputable facts."

"That might be true," Nonce replied. "But who has the real power here?"

"If you are speaking literally for once, then the answer is obvious." Uncouth had that petulant tone I last heard when he lost his argument with Eade.

"Exactly." I could hear the smirk in Nonce's voice. "Now, go down there and find out who is interfering in Knotstick business."

"We should wait for one of those engineers." Uncouth sounded like he wasn't keen on descending the sloping tunnel on his own.

"Why? Afraid of ghosts?" Nonce's smirk was like a shout.

"Of course I'm not afraid. It's more an instinctive aversion to going into dark tunnels where dead people have been lying about for centuries."

"Arthur's underwear," Nonce muttered. "Fine, follow me."

CHAPTER 32

Embarrassment isn't the sort of thing you normally consider as having a physical mass. It creates intense emotions and anxiety, sure. But to physically manifest as its own thing is not normal, no matter how much you wish the ground would open up and swallow you. Fortunately, normal and I had done little more than exchange Hibernian Season's Greetings cards in quite a while.

In a final moment of desperation, with nowhere to hide and Drakeforth bent over and staring at the floor while he paced up and down like a chicken with a dowsing rod, I leaned against the empathic energy engine and assumed an air of casual nonchalance, so cool you could have chilled drinks on my head.

Erskine and Nonce came bustling into the chamber. Goat froze in place. Eade hunkered down beside the engine, while Drakeforth ignored the new arrivals. I gave them a nod, as if acknowledging the arrival of old friends at a bar.

The two men gaped at us, harrumphed, bargled, and went several shades of *punk*, that mysterious colour between pink and purple.

"Hey," I said with an effortless attempt at a wave.

"What...? Who...? What...?" Based on his facial contortions, Erskine appeared to be a man at war with himself, and casualties were mounting.

"Eade Notschnott?" Nonce asked.

"Possibly," Eade said.

"What are you people doing? This is a most sacred place. It's forbidden to be in here!" Nonce exploded.

"Well," I said with an unaccustomed icy calm, "I'm a tourist. I was sightseeing."

"Forbidden!" Nonce squeaked.

"I have some experience with vintage empathy machines," I continued. "This little beauty—" I paused to pat the humming chrome cylinder as if it was a large, friendly dog, "—is a Godden Model Six."

"Model Four," Erskine snapped.

"Really?" I stepped away and studied the machine. "I could have sworn it was a six."

"Nope, four. It has the original brass valve plating on the moderator housing and the three-quarter inch inlay pipe on the flux inhibitor."

"Yeah, of course. How did I miss that?" I nodded, with absolutely no clue what he was talking about.

Nonce noticed Goat standing rigid against the wall. Both of them gave a start and then immediately looked away.

"You cannot be here," Nonce insisted.

"I wonder why?" I asked no one in particular. "Could it be the unexplainable presence of a Godden empathy engine in the middle of a Pathian pyramid?"

"There are no devices of an empathic nature in Pathia," Nonce intoned.

"Except the murrai?" I replied.

"There is no evidence that murrai are empathically empowered," Nonce shouted.

"Of course they are!" I slapped my thighs in frustration. "They positively sizzle with empathic energy!"

Nonce cleared his throat. "Erskine…" he said with the tone of a spouse warning their significant other that later there is going to be one Balkans of a row.

"Oh yes," Erskine flinched. "You need to explain yourself. Yourselves, all of you."

"Charlotte Pudding. Tourist," I repeated. "This is my friend, Vole Drakeforth, his ex-wife Eade Notschnott, who I think you know quite well, Mr Uncouth. This ahh… fellow, is Goat. Our tour-guide and driver."

Goat gave a self-conscious wave.

Nonce had been fingering a rod-like pendant around his neck. It looked old and inappropriate, which meant it had to be a religious symbol of some kind. He took a step back and put the end of the thing in his mouth, blowing until his cheeks puffed. I heard nothing and wondered if it was like a dog-whistle, except the silent blast of energy that echoed across the chamber rocked me on my feet.

"It's taken care of," Nonce said. Uncouth flinched again and backed out of the chamber.

"What did you just do?" I demanded, and Nonce raised an eyebrow.

"Whatever do you mean?"

"You blew that whistle thing, and something happened."

"This is a *sibilus*, a symbol of my esteemed position in the Knotstick Order."

"Really? I could have sworn it was some kind of whistle."

Nonce stared at me with an adze-worth of flint in his glare. "Erksine, we are leaving," he announced, and vanished up the passageway to the surface.

Uncouth hesitated as if he wanted to apologise, explain, or invite us to a kitchenware buying party; instead, he gave a whimper and scuttled after Nonce.

"Well, that was unpleasant," I said. Drakeforth was now on his hands and knees, seemingly measuring the floor with his fingers and blowing dust from the fine gaps between the heavy blocks of sandstone.

"We should get out of here, immediately." Eade stood and in an ultimately futile gesture, she dusted the dust from her knees.

"Agreed." I started for the door and the lights went out.

CHAPTER 33

"Morning!" Goat said cheerfully in the dark.

"Eade, do you happen to have a light?" I asked, not daring to move.

"You know, I told myself before I left that floating shack earlier, the last thing I must do is leave my phone behind."

"And?" I asked through gritted teeth.

"It was actually the second to last thing I did."

"Wonderful." I did have a mobile phone. Somewhere. I tended not to carry it with me in case someone tried to call me on it.

"What can I get everyone for breakfast?" Goat burbled. "Sorry, there's not much variety."

"Drakeforth?"

"Yes, Pudding?"

"Did they close the door to the pyramid, effectively sealing us in here and leaving us to die slowly of asphyxiation and dehydration?"

"It seems like the simplest solution to their problem," Drakeforth replied.

"Real go-getters, those two," Eade said.

"Drakeforth, is there some way I could die now and save the wait? The idea of three days listening to Eade makes me long for the oblivion of death."

"You sure that death and oblivion are the same thing?" Drakeforth sounded closer. I wanted to reach out and find him, but the thought of actually touching someone unexpectedly in the dark made me recoil internally.

I stiffened as Drakeforth clamped a hand around my arm. "Come with me," he said.

"You'll have to guide me. I seem to have forgotten how to open my eyes."

Drakeforth pulled me forward several steps, Then shuffled me sideways, and finally we turned ninety-degrees.

"You dance divinely," I said, grinning in the dark where no one could see.

"Next time you can lead," Drakeforth replied. "This is the spot. Do your thing."

"Which thing?"

"We are standing on top of a large reservoir of unrefined double-e flux. I would like you to encourage it to blast a hole in the side of this fabrication of fraudulence."

"Right, now how should I do that?"

"You did it before."

"That was a different circumstance. Our lives were threatened."

"What makes you think our lives aren't threatened now?" Drakeforth asked.

"My sense of urgency is not feeling it."

"Have you tried explaining the gravity of our situation to your sense of urgency?" Drakeforth asked.

"I could, but it's more of a crisis thing. Not a slow build up to worst-case scenario."

"How have you have managed to live this long should be the focus of in-depth study."

"Perhaps they could make a documentary," I said into the dark.

"If you're interested," Eade said in a tone that suggested our interest was the least of her priorities, "the stone block that was blocking the entrance is, once again, blocking the entrance."

"They might make a documentary about us, 'The Mystery of the Bodies Found in the Pyramid'," I suggested.

"Someone will say it was aliens," Drakeforth replied. "Can you feel it?"

"Feel what?" The grit beneath my shoes felt like popping candy in my mouth.

"Empathic energy. Bustling about under your feet like it has something important to do."

"Uh-huh." The stone felt like hot sand. The darkness sparkled and light started glowing in a pattern across the floor.

"We should get out of here," I muttered.

"That's the plan," Drakeforth said, stepping back.

"Vole!" Eade yelled. "Do we simply have to die in here?"

"Pudding is taking care of it," Vole said. I appreciated his confidence. It stood out in stark contrast to the complete lack of my own.

Right. Take care of it, Pudding. I tried to recall the awful occasion when the latest in a series of Godden's despicably artificial descendants almost ruined my life. A tumult of empathic energy had poured through me in that corporate office over a production line of assimilation agents. *How did you feel?* I asked myself. *Very angry. Very scared. Very…tired.* I checked my current status. *Annoyed. Uneasy and very tired.*

"How's she getting on, do you think?" Eade asked, loud enough for the murrai outside to hear.

"The room hasn't exploded, so I'd say she's still warming up," Drakeforth replied.

"Exploded?" Eade asked. "Why in the colander would the room explode?"

I wanted to yell, *"Because you won't shut up and you are annoying the tardigrades out of me!"* Instead, the floor collapsed and I fell into a whirlpool rainbow of chaotic emotions.

CHAPTER 34

The idea of an afterlife is a cornerstone of many religions. It's the faith equivalent of "eat your vegetables, and you'll get something nice for dessert". Drakeforth, of course railed against organised religion. He went out of his way to accost and annoy his own followers, and if he met anyone with a different system of belief, he would probably unload his insults on them, too. I wondered if he would show respect to the actually deceased. He would probably appreciate that they didn't interrupt him when he was ranting.

I floated in a warm glow of feelings. *The pure distillation of life. Fragments of experience. Slivers of memory. Shards of despair and dandruff flakes of joy.* I did not sink, though at the same time I didn't backstroke and squirt sparkling empathic energy into the air, either. I was a synchronised swimmer without a team. Just me and a legion of spectator moments swirling like a tornado of confused fish.

My intake of breath sparkled and fizzed.

"I know," I said. "I mean, I don't know. I haven't been where you are. Or aren't."

I fell silent; even in conversation with the dead, my lack of social skills made me want to shrivel up.

A tear, a freckle, the glint of an eye. An amalgam of fractal features came together. A thousand pieces of people formed into what could have been a single face. For a moment, it looked like Dad.

"Marzipan," he might have whispered, and the echo rippled through the ether.

"Me?" Of course *me*. There was no one else here, and while everyone called me Charlotte, except for Drakeforth, who insisted on that faux-formality of calling me by my last name, I might have misheard the word. Dad had never called me *Marzipan*, for which I was grateful.

The face folded into the kaleidoscope of double-e flux. If there were others, I didn't recognise them.

I continued doing the equivalent of treading water while I waited for Drakeforth to do something. He was probably making a rope out of Goat's nasal hair to lift me out. I didn't seem at imminent risk of drowning, so hanging around—floating, for want of a better description—was all I could do.

"Is there anything I can do?" I asked somewhat tardily.

Immersion in empathic energy is unlike anything else. For most people it is about as distressing as being dipped into a nightclub light show. Lots of pretty colours, but no physical effects other than maybe a little retina burn.

The fine hairs on my arms waved like sea-grass at high tide as whatever I was breathing sparkled and tingled in my lungs.

With a burning sense of self-consciousness, I started to make swimming motions. It worked better than I had hoped, and I half floated and half swam through a glowing mist that both curled towards my full attention and recoiled from my touch. It was like moving through the personalities of cats.

The swirling mist cleared to sparkly murk and I felt something almost solid under my feet. I experienced the total calm akin to being the only person in a bouncy castle moments before some annoying kids come in shrieking and throwing themselves into the wall.

Landscapes require a lot of work: ask any artist or professional gardener. The scene forming before my eyes had incredible detail, from the cloud-like ground to the sweeping lines of the tree that dominated my view.

She swept into view astride a rope-and-board swing that hung from the tree—head back, legs outstretched, black hair streaming like a comet's tail as she arced through the air.

I kept quiet and watched her fly, my stomach doing flip-flops as she sailed through the amplitude of the pendulum swing.

"You're late," a gruff voice said.

I jumped and felt the ground bounce gently under me. "Wha?! Oo?! Wherg?!" I babbled.

"I said, you are late. Professor Polis Bombilate, and I'm not entirely sure to be honest."

"Are you dead?" The question came out before I had time to think of something more polite to ask.

"Aren't we all? Eventually, I mean." Bombilate shrugged.

"Sorry," I apologised, realising what I had said sounded quite rude.

"No point in apologising. You're here now. Which is better than where you were a minute ago. With any luck you will find me and stop these fractured finger flappers before they ruin everything."

"Finger?" I frowned.

"Excuse my strong language," Bombilate said.

"Wait... Ruin everything?"

"Yes. Everything. You should hurry up and find me."

"Where are you!?"

"If I knew that, don't you think I would have led with it?"

"I hardly know you! But yes! That would make sense!"

"Good. See you soon." Bombilate faded in a swirl of empathic energy.

"If it's all the same to you, I'd be happy to stay here!" I said.

"Wake up, Pudding! We can't stay here." Drakeforth shook me and I blinked. The stone chamber of the pyramid came into sharp focus.

"I saw Professor Bombilate!" I was yelling over the noise of the Godden engine whining as it red-lined its RPMs or whatever engines did when they made a noise like a boulder going through a bandsaw.

"Great!" Drakeforth yelled. "It will be nice to feel we achieved something in this, the last moments of our lives!"

"What's going on!?" A fine dust was drifting down through the cracks, and the stones around us vibrated.

"Well!" Drakeforth bellowed, "It's a long story, but if you

really want me to tell you, I will try to get to the point before we are crushed to a pulp!"

Goat and Eade were pushing against a block of stone that fitted perfectly into the space where the entrance had been earlier.

The woman with black hair stood unmoving in the centre of the room, a black umbrella open over her head as dust and gravel rained down on it and bounced away as easily as rain.

"We need to leave!" I yelled.

Drakeforth gave me a long-suffering look that stung worse than his anger. "You think?" He managed to shout the question and make it sarcastic at the same time.

Empathic energy flowed around us. Every time I moved my hands or ducked under a stream of dust, everything blurred in a rainbow of light. I could see beyond the stone walls. Through the pulsing reservoir of energy that was deeper and stronger than anything I had ever seen. All the way to the shining light of the murrai. Standing outside the pyramid, the heavy stone block was now being pushed back into place by their masonry hands.

"I think I can help…" My voice was blurred and distorted. The slow grind of stone machines deep in the belly of the pyramid made everything vibrate. I looked past Drakeforth, Eade, and Goat, who wore glowing auras of colourful sparks. I reached through the vibrating strings of reality to where the murrai stood, mute and patient outside of the pyramid.

"Open the way," I instructed. They didn't move. "Please?" I tried again. Nothing. What was it Drakeforth said? Murrai are machines? Just because they were made to look like people didn't make them people. They were tools. As simple as hammers.

I mentally slapped myself, took a deep breath and punched the air. The murrai' stone fists smashed into the rock. It cracked with a puff of dust. I adjusted my feet and struck again, slamming my fist into the wall.

"Ow! Fruit!" I swore.

Shaking my skinned knuckles, I struck again, careful to pull my punch this time. The murrai showed no such restraint. In two blows from their massive stone fists, the block in front of me fell apart. The force of it sent chunks of rock spinning and bouncing across the chamber floor, and dust dancing through the air. The murrai stood silhouetted in the dusk as we staggered out coughing and choking in the dusty air.

"What in the hindquarters just happened?" Eade asked as she wiped dust from her eyes.

"Empathic energy overload, I suspect," Drakeforth said. "Sound right to you, Pudding?"

"Yargh," I spat. "The way the flux capacitor was running in there, they must be doing an emergency purge of the storage tanks and the system couldn't handle the positive pressure."

"It's not the usual reference work, but it will do in a pinch," Goat said.

Behind us, the machine howled and sent arcs of electricity crawling up the walls like the legs of neon spiders.

"We should keep moving. This place could still light up like a whale full of glow-shrimp." Drakeforth took Eade and me by the arms, and hurried down the stone steps of the pyramid.

"I think I saw Professor Bombilate," I said, while focusing on finding the next step down the steep slope as we rushed.

"What? In there?" Eade half turned and looked back. The stone doorway we had just left vented an explosion of double-e flux. A tornado in metallic rainbow colours erupted out of the side of the pyramid with the roar of a volcano vomiting.

"Kinda?" I suggested.

"Plenty of time to talk about that when we aren't in danger — when we are in less danger than we currently are," Drakeforth said. He picked up the pace, and we were soon running down the stone steps. Chunks of carefully placed sandstone block crashed down around us. The smaller bits fell like rain, with the thunder of the storm behind us.

"This isn't like last time," I gasped.

"Oh? Does this happen to you often?" Eade managed to be sarcastic and pant in terror at the same time.

"Duck," Drakeforth announced. We did, and a murrai somersaulted over our heads, hit the steps and bounced down towards the sand, loose as a flying snake.

In this moment of complete helplessness, I found my mind

very clear. "Last time," I continued as if Eade and the tumbling murrai hadn't interrupted me, "there was a massive explosion, and it was relatively silent. This one is loud enough to wake the de—the very deep sleepers. I was thinking it might be due to the acoustics. All that energy pushing though a narrow hole in the side of the pyramid, blowing a lot of air with it."

"What the strawberry is she on about?!" Eade yelled.

"It's an interesting theory," Drakeforth replied. "Empathic energy contains a great deal of quantum energy, but it's not very reactive at a larger scale. Under sufficient pressure, who knows what it might do?"

"Surely, Arthur would?" I wanted to make it sound casual, but I ran into the sand at the bottom of the pyramid and fell flat on my face.

CHAPTER 35

Goat's airship floated in the wash of the disintegrating pyramid. We scrambled up the goat-hide ropes and cast off. This mostly involved Goat running around and pulling on levers while the rest of us took half steps and made ineffectual offers of assistance.

"Perhaps I should make us all a cup of tea?" Drakeforth suggested.

"Oh please... If you want us to drink it, then I'll make it." Eade walked off to the kitchen before either of us could compose a suitable comeback or an explanation for why she suddenly fell overboard.

"What did you see?" Drakeforth asked, his face looking quite sickly in the shimmering glow of the pyramid that was still erupting.

"I'm not sure. There was a lot of empathic energy. I was floating in a thousand lives. All fragments. Then I saw the tree, and she was on a swing. Then Professor Bombilate appeared and told me to find him."

"Excellent. Where exactly did he say to find him?"

"If I knew that, don't you think I would have led with it?"

"I thought you might be working on building dramatic tension."

"I have no idea where he is," I admitted.

"What do we know? You have a fascinating ability to interact with empathic energy. You had a vision of sorts featuring Professor Bombilate and The Tree."

"And her," I replied.

"You saw some odd things while under the influence of the double-e flux, and you saw Professor Bombilate."

"Yes, which is odd, because I don't know the man at all."

"That *is* odd. He is the leading authority on infornomics in the world. I thought you might have at least read something about him."

"I have this weird quirk where I don't read every single article or book ever written about every single thing. Computer psychology? I'm your expert. The Cragmark film franchise? I was a member of the fan club from the age of seven."

"They made nineteen of those sensies, didn't they?" Drakeforth asked.

"Technically, they made sixteen. The last three were a spinoff attempt at a reboot, which upset many of us hardcore Craggers. A large number of angry forum posts were made on that subject, I can assure you."

"A tragedy for the entire entertainment industry." Drakeforth nodded sympathetically, which made my eyes narrow.

"You can be sarcastic about many things, Drakeforth. Just keep your snide remarks about the single greatest story ever told to yourself."

"If someone wishes to immerse themselves in a virtual reality experience for hours at a time, then who am I to judge?"

"You cannot be serious. You judge everyone and everything!"

Drakeforth did his best to beam at me. "Precisely."

"That's it!" I did a dance that was more like a convulsion. "I know where to find Professor Bombilate!"

Drakeforth regarded me steadily; I could almost see him replaying the conversation in his head.

"I was immersed in empathic energy. The tiny flakes of the life force of all those people. Who knows how many they have been pumping into the pyramid?"

"Yes, yes, generations of people, I am sure," Drakeforth ushered me along to the point.

"Bombilate was entire. He was whole. He stood there and talked to me."

"Which means he's still in one piece. Possibly still alive even…"

Drakeforth took a deep breath. "Pudding, there are moments when you almost give me hope for the future of humanity."

"Don't get all squishy on me now, Drakeforth."

"Where in all of Pathia would they be keeping him?"

I looked out at the sparkling remnants of the pyramid summit. We were hardly making a fast getaway in this drifting wreck. "Remember the tank at the monastery? The one where the old sisters and brothers went when they were ready to die? We need to find an extraction tank like that. It must be what they are doing with Bombilate."

"You think the professor sacrificed himself to some secret cult of Arthurians?" Drakeforth asked.

"It's the only thing that makes any sense," I said.

"It's the only thing that makes any sense?" Drakeforth echoed. "Pudding, have you taken complete leave of your senses?"

"Yes!" I slapped my thigh and danced an impromptu interpretive thing. "I got you! I finally got you! I said something sarcastic and you completely fell for it!"

"What if you're right?" Drakeforth interrupted my victory celebration.

"Have you taken complete—? Wait… That's not fair. I got you."

"How often do things that make no sense actually prove to be true?"

"Nev— Well hardly ev— Sometime—" I fell silent. "It's still the stupidest thing I have ever heard."

"You said it," Drakeforth replied.

"I was joking!"

"It doesn't mean it's not true."

"Where would they hide something like that in Pathia?"

Drakeforth looked to the pyramid. The fountain of glittering energy gushing from it had subsided, and various emergency services were converging on the area with a jarring disharmony of sirens and flashing lights.

"In there?" I asked.

"Why not? Close to the storage system for their ill-gotten gains."

"We should go back, have a good look around."

"Did you just say we should go back and get arrested?"

"What? No?"

"Weird, because that is exactly what 'go back and have a good look around' sounds like."

"We can't just leave," I said as the lights flashing about made the shadows of the ship dance.

"Leaving is what Drakeforth is best at," Eade announced, setting down a battered tray of full cups.

"Where's Goat?" Eade asked.

I think he's up in the wriggling," I said waving in the general direction of the macramé maze of knotted ropes and cords that seemed to be important in holding the mass of inflated goat-intestines together.

"Rigging," Eade said, and sipped her tea.

I drank a mouthful of hot tea to stop me snapping at her, and a helicopter thudded into our airspace, fingers of searing white light stabbing at the deck before steadying and pinning us under their thumbs.

"Act natural," Drakeforth warned.

"That is possibly the worst advice I have heard in a long time," I muttered.

An amplified voice boomed over the rotor wash. "You! On the—the—whatever that is! Land immediately and prepare to be boarded!"

Goat bounced through the rigging like a fly trying to get through a closed window. The spotlight left us and chased him; he whooped and howled before leaping for a thick plaited cord and dragging it down to the deck in slow motion. A ripping, gaseous noise echoed through the night air. The stink of it made me gag. Drakeforth covered his face and Eade turned green.

A cloud of stinking warm gas exhaled in a loose-lipped flubbering from the net of balloons. We slowly slipped towards the ground, settling on the sand like a beached ship.

People in uniforms circled the ship. We did not assist them in getting on board; however, they managed themselves well enough.

Goat insisted on shaking the various officers' hands and seemed to be offering them tea. Four of them tackled him to the deck and handcuffed his wrists behind his back. Then they advanced on us.

"You are all under arrest," the first officer announced.

"On what charge?" Drakeforth asked.

"We are still writing a list. I can assure you it is comprehensive and long."

"We are innocent of all charges," Drakeforth replied.

"Of course you are. We have to prove you are guilty. Until then you are entirely innocent," the officer nodded.

"So we can go, then?" I asked with a sudden surge of hope.

"Not on your life," the officer replied. "Escort these suspects to detention. They will be held for questioning and forensic examination."

"Forensic examination? Doesn't that require us to be dead?" I asked.

The officer shrugged. "Depends entirely on how cooperative you are during questioning."

"I'm a tourist! You can't arrest me!" I squeaked.

"Of course we can't." The officer gestured to a companion and they pulled my arms back and handcuffed me.

"A mugshot will look great in the holiday album—if you ever get out of jail, that is," the officer said.

"Don't tell them anything, Pudding," Drakeforth warned.

"I don't know anything!" I managed to shout over the noise.

"That's the idea!" Drakeforth yelled back.

Eade and Goat were already in the back seat of a 4WD with cartoonishly large balloon tyres. We were shoved inside and the doors closed, bringing air-conditioned silence to the night.

"Geese are terrifying," Goat suddenly blurted. Eade stared at him, her face an unpleasant mix of confusion and pity. Goat looked confused and went back to staring out the window.

Someone banged on the roof and the vehicle roared to life. It sounded like a large predatory animal in full rut. It took me a moment to realise that this is what an engine burning fossil fuel must sound like.

"I can see why they soundproof their vehicles," I said.

Drakeforth closed his eyes. "The lengths to which some cultures will go to avoid using empathic energy are quite extreme."

"Not as extreme as the lengths cultures using empathic energy will go," I replied, and closed my eyes against the flashing lights.

CHAPTER 36

had never been in a jail cell before, and the novelty wore off even faster than I thought it would.

They are all the same, really: a simple secure box with a locked cage door on one side, a bed with a mattress thinner than processed cheese slices and a toilet that was the most basic item in a catalogue without any of the bonus features.

We took turns sitting on the bed and turns pacing up and down the small cell (nine steps each way for me) and turns leaning against the stone wall and staring at the floor.

I was on my third round of staring at the floor when a uniformed officer unlocked the door.

"You," he pointed at me. "Out."

"I want my phone call," I said.

"Sure, who would you like us to contact?"

"I don't know, the embassy?"

"Are you a diplomat or government official of a foreign power?"

"Uhm, no?"

"Out."

I left the cell, relieved to be able to walk further than the length of my bathroom for the first time in hours.

"This way." He indicated the exit. I walked meekly to the door. From there it was a short walk to an interview room, which was like the cell, except without the bespoke interior design elements.

"Sit down," the officer instructed. I took a seat opposite a table that looked like it had been carved from the same concrete block as the room and the chairs.

I waited in the room alone for a while. We hadn't talked about alibis or gotten our stories straight. I felt certain that Eade would be spilling her beans, telling the lawn everything, laying the blame squarely at the feet of Drakeforth and myself.

The door opened and a woman in a suit walked in. She closed the door and sat down opposite me.

"I'm Inquisitor Cartouche." The Inquisitor had a gentle, mother-ly sense about her. I bet she made criminals feel like lying to her would be like lying to their mums.

"Hello," I said meekly.

"Do you know why I have asked you to come and talk to me today?" she asked.

"Lysteria started it!" I said, and immediately winced.

"Did she?" Inquisitor Cartouche didn't have a pen and wasn't recording the conversation. I felt relieved about that. "Which one is Lysteria?" she asked.

"Sorry, it just came out. Lysteria Esconce was a girl I knew in high school. I haven't seen her in years. I was just thinking about the one time I got called to the headmistress's office, and it was definitely Lysteria's fault."

"Perhaps we could start with your name?" Cartouche asked in that same gentle tone.

"Charlotte Pudding," I replied immediately.

"Why are you in Pathia, Miss Pudding?"

"Holiday. It's such a fascinating country. The pyramids, the sand, the fossil fuel smoke. So much to see and experience."

"How did you come to be near the pyramid earlier this evening?"

I half laughed. "It's a long story," I said, waving the question away. Inquisitor Cartouche stared at me, unblinking as a murrai. "I love a long story."

"Do you?" I looked at her, my desperation not to engage in lengthy conversation evident in my expression.

"How did you come to be at the pyramid earlier this evening?" Cartouche asked again.

"We got there on Goat's airship. It's an odd thing. Built from scrap and parts that might once have been spare. It's some kind of balloon. Except he uses inflated goat intestines all tied together to give it lift."

"Quite the feat of engineering," Cartouche said.

"I suppose."

"Why did he build this balloon craft?"

"Honestly, I have no idea. I mean, he seems nice enough, but he's not quite working on the same day's crossword as the rest of us, you know?"

"There have been reports that this floating ship was brought to the site by two murrai," Cartouche said gently.

"Yeah, how weird is that?" I was so used to feeling guilty that when I finally had a reason to look guilty, I wondered what my face must look like.

"Very strange. Murrai are the property of the Knotstick church. It's unusual to see them wandering about unless they are under the direct control of a Knotstick priest."

"How do they control them?"

Cartouche stared at me in a way that felt like being sized up by a soft toy filled with spiders. "They have always controlled them."

I took a deep breath, and said, "The pyramid is full of double-e flux. Empathic energy. You know, the stuff that Pathia hasn't used as an energy source in hundreds of years? We think the Knotstick church is using the pyramids as a storage facility and probably selling off the energy to the Godden Corporation, who incidentally are not the benefactors of all mankind they want you to believe."

"Why did you blow up the pyramid?" Cartouche asked.

"I didn't! I mean…I don't think I did."

"You were there. The pyramid was badly damaged in what has been reported by eyewitnesses as an explosion. What kind of explosives did you use?"

"Frustration, annoyance and a whole lot of panic at the thought of my impending death," I explained.

"Were you forced to detonate the explosives?"

"There were no explosives. The pyramid itself is full of empathic energy. That is what blew up."

"There is no empathic energy in Pathia," Cartouche reminded me.

"What are the murrai running on, then?"

"Faith," Cartouche said. "The faith of the Knotstick church drives the machines. It is a miracle."

"Are you planning on telling Drakeforth that?" I asked.

"Which one is Drakeforth?"

"The tall one with the coat and the arrogant aura."

"Is he a man of faith?" Cartouche asked.

My giggle came out at a pitch high enough to sound hysterical. "You could say that."

"How long have you been part of the Credit Union?"

"Sorry, the what?"

"The Credit Union. We know they are active in the city. Several cells have been under surveillance for some time. You've certainly raised the stakes by committing this act of vandalism."

"Wait." I resisted the urge to put my hand up at knowing the answer to a question by knotting my fingers together in my lap. "Eade, the blonde woman, she told me about some terrorist organisation called the Credit Union. I saw their symbol on the wall outside our hotel. It looked like..." I went to rummage in my pockets and then remembered that the officers took everything off me when they checked us in. "It looked like a credit stick," I finished.

"Why did the Union destroy the pyramid?" Cartouche asked.

"They didn't—" I caught myself. "I don't know anything about this terrorist bank or whatever they are. I just know that they didn't blow it up."

"Because you did?" the inquisitor asked.

"Kinda?" I tried.

"The others, how are they involved?"

"Drakeforth is actually inhabited, possessed I guess, by the immortal spirit of Arthur. Eade Notschnott is Drakeforth's ex-wife and she asked him to come here and help her find Professor Bombilate. Goat, we met by chance."

"That's why they are involved," the inquisitor said.

"Is it?"

"Yes."

"And?"

"It wasn't the question I asked."

"It wasn't?"

"Tell me about the last time you were questioned by an officer of the lore," she said.

"This is a first for me," I admitted.

"You are very good at saying a lot without actually saying anything. What do you do for a job?"

"I'm a computer psychologist. I studied dialectics in university as well."

"Curious."

"Not overly. I'd much prefer to stay home and watch it on the telly."

"I mean it's a curious combination of skill sets. Quite useful in avoiding answering questions, I imagine."

I smiled thinly. "We don't always get to choose our roles in the scheme of things."

"Do you regret it?"

"The lack of choice, or my role in the scheme of things?"

"What do you regret?"

I fell silent. Regrets are like stamps: some people collect them obsessively while others acquire them and then send them on. I seemed to find regrets at the oddest moments, like a half-used book of stamps in a desk drawer.

"No regrets," I said eventually. "Plenty of things I would do differently, I guess."

"You wish you hadn't destroyed the ancient pyramid?"

"I wish the pyramid hadn't been destroyed. I didn't destroy it. *We* destroyed it. By that I mean everyone. People like you, the Knotstick church...Erskine Uncouth, that guy, Nonce—"

"You are accusing Grand Linteum Nonce of being involved in the plot to destroy the pyramid?"

"Is he the guy with the whistle? He called it a...*syllabus*?"

"Sibilus. It is the sacred symbol of the Knotstick Order."

"It's a whistle that controls murrai," I countered.

"The purpose and rituals of the Order are not for us to understand," Cartouche snapped.

"It's exactly that kind of insistence on ignorance that got us here in the first place!"

The door opened and a uniformed officer stepped into the room. He walked over to Inquisitor Cartouche and whispered something in her ear, before leaving as uselessly as he had arrived.

"This interview is terminated," Cartouche announced. She stood up and opened the door. "You will be returned to your cell."

"I am sure I reserved a private room on the booking," I said as I stepped out into the stone hallway.

"Charlotte Pudding?" A man in a white, four-piece suit regarded me intently.

"Yes?"

"Dollar William; I am your legal representation. You will be pleased to know I have arranged for your release."

"Okay?"

"Come with me please." William offered to take my arm, which I declined by shying away from him. He indicated the exit sign at the far end of the corridor. "Your friends are waiting for you."

"I expect we will be seeing each other again soon, Miss Pudding," Cartouche said calmly.

"Thanks for having me, you have been most hospitable." I almost curtsied to the inquisitor and then hurried for the exit.

CHAPTER 37

It was still dark outside, which meant we hadn't been in custody for as long as it felt. Or it meant we had been in custody for days, which it definitely felt like.

William guided me to a sand coloured van, the kind of vehicle widely used by tradespeople and kidnappers around the world. The side door slid open, a dark shape lunged out and a cloth bag was pulled over my head as they bundled me inside.

"This really isn't necessary," I said through the muffling fabric.

"Welcome aboard, Pudding," Drakeforth said from somewhere nearby. "Our mystery tour is about to begin."

"Quiet," William said, and it sounded like he thumped Drakeforth.

"The key," Goat said and I could almost hear him nodding.

The engine roared into life and we careened through the narrow streets. Inside the van, I struggled to stay in my seat as we took corners at tyre-squealing speed.

"Where did you study law?" I asked.

"Quiet," William replied.

"I only ask, because this is my first time actually needing a lawyer to get me out of jail, and it does seem a little odd to be shoved into an unmarked van with a bag over my head."

"I won't tell you again, keep quiet."

"Hit her and you will regret it," Drakeforth said.

Everyone fell silent and the van stampeded on through the city.

We would arrive at our destination eventually, though resigning myself to the inevitable set my teeth on edge. I felt powerless and angry. So I waited, feeling determined to inflict as much inconvenience on our captors' lives as possible, when the time was right.

The van slowed and stopped, engine growling like my stomach. How long had it been since I ate? After a pause, we rolled forward and stopped. The engine went silent and a door rolled down behind us.

We were guided out of the van and my bag was removed. I blinked at the space. Some kind of cavernous room, perhaps a warehouse. A large rug marked an attempt at making some kind of lounge, complete with furniture and table decorations. The van had parked in the middle of the floor, and a small group of people regarded us suspiciously. I glared back at them, pleased to have a target for my annoyance.

I looked to my left, where Drakeforth and Eade stood, dishevelled and bagless. I could smell Goat to my right.

Dollar William came into view. "You have questions, and I may have answers. I also have food if you are hungry. Come and make yourselves comfortable."

We took seats in soft couches and I accepted a plate with a fresh sandwich without saying thank you. *That will show them.*

"Welcome to the Credit Union," William said.

"You bologna-biting-belligerents," Drakeforth said.

"Drakeforth, don't insult people with your mouth full," Eade chided.

I finished chewing and asked, "Where's Professor Bombilate?"

William frowned. "We were going to ask you the same thing."

"You kidnapped him and us," I replied.

"We did not kidnap anyone. We lost Bombilate and we rescued you from our oppressors."

"Doesn't that make you our oppressors?" I asked.

William raised an eyebrow and turned slightly to check our surroundings. "Do you feel oppressed?"

"I feel a lot of things; oppressed is pretty far down the list," I admitted, and took another sandwich.

"Why are we here?" Eade asked.

"You took affirmative action against the forces that seek to enslave all of Pathia," William replied.

"You think we blew up the pyramid on purpose?" I asked. "That's exactly what the lawn thought, too."

"Lawn?"

"Yeah, the police. Where I come from, they wear green uniforms. We call them *The Lawn*." I sounded way more gangster than I felt.

"You were explaining why we have been freed from legal imprisonment, recklessly driven through the streets, and finally fed sandwiches," Eade said.

"Really good sandwiches." My plan to make them all suffer was fading with my hunger.

"Thank you, and yes I was, wasn't I?" William replied. "Why did you blow up the pyramid?"

"We didn't! At least not on purpose." I felt that I was covering well-trod ground. "Is this some kind of trick? You're actually police and trying to get us to admit to something we didn't do?"

"I can assure you that we are as far from officers of the lore as you are from home," William said.

"Drakeforth, what do you think?" I asked.

"I think I will have another sandwich while you tell them everything" Drakeforth replied.

CHAPTER 38

I hadn't talked that much in a long time and when I finally stopped, the room remained silent. Eade was frowning deeply and Goat appeared to be asleep.

"Quite the story," William said, rousing himself from a near trance.

"It's all true." I stifled a yawn. Performance art was exhausting. Even if it was just telling the story of my recent life's upheavals to a bunch of economic revolutionaries.

"Empathic energy…" William said. "Well, that just proves what we have been saying all along."

"Surely that depends on what you have been saying all along?" Eade replied.

William spoke with the certainty of a zealot who has memorised his dogma: "The current knowledge economy is an unsustainable model of economic management. The entire country is hurtling towards a complete breakdown of social order."

"Yes, clearly there is chaos in the streets," Eade said.

"It is coming," William replied with smug certainty.

"And you think the only way to save Pathia is to switch to the credit system used elsewhere?" Eade asked.

"It's the only option that makes sense," William replied. "Tourism, exports, technology… We can leave the sandstone age ideals behind and embrace the modern world."

I closed my eyes and took a deep breath. "The modern world runs on empathic energy, and if you missed the big bit in the middle of my story, I did explain that the primary source of that energy is dead people."

"Hardly our problem, Pathia doesn't use empathic energy." William waved my concerns away like a heretic swatting a fly.

"We are talking about people, actual people. The energy of their existence being ground up and used to power toaster-ovens."

"Not around here," William insisted.

"Except, maybe, you know, the pyramid that was stuffed full of the stuff?" I replied.

"Which has nothing to do with actually using empathic energy," William continued. "We want to change the economic system, not get tangled up in the ethics of an unnecessary alternative energy system."

"You're putting profits before people?" I felt quite shocked by the casual dismissal of all those lives.

"Yes, exactly." William seemed pleased that I understood.

"If you changed the system, would you allow the Godden Energy Corporation to export and sell double-e flux extracted from Pathian citizens?" I asked.

"If they were prepared to pay for what they harvest, then sure," William replied.

"Okay, I've heard enough: you are terrorists. This entire country really takes the toupee."

"We still need your help to find Professor Bombilate," William replied.

"What do you want with the professor?" Eade demanded.

"Isn't it obvious? Bombilate knows the truth. He was working with us to bring about the economic revolution."

Eade gave a harsh, barking laugh.

"Nonsense!" She stood up and paced around the lounge set like she was performing a one act play in one of those tiny theatres where there is no more than six inches between the edge of your seat and the row in front. "Professor Bombilate is the leading authority on infornomics. Not only has he written and lectured extensively about the benefits and strength of the knowledge economy, he has also shown that it is the best system for a stable society."

"Odd, isn't it?" Drakeforth commented casually. "Two extremists with different views, and yet they are both utterly certain of the irrefutable nature of their world view."

"It's like one of those rom-com sensies," I said. "The two characters are at opposite extremes, they hate each other and everything the other stands for, then they end up falling in love and their opposing ideologies are completely abandoned in the final act."

"Compromise is when both parties lose," Drakeforth replied.

I glanced at Eade, who was fully engaged in arguing with William. "Only if you have never truly been in love."

"Marriage for a work permit does not require love," Drakeforth said.

"You must have felt something?" I asked.

"Relief, mostly," Drakeforth replied in a tone that suggested he was done talking about it.

"Compromise. Maybe that is what we need." I stood up and waited for a gap in the argument to interrupt.

"I know where Professor Bombilate is!" I shouted over the rising voices.

"What? Where?" Eade turned in mid-rant and held a hand up to silence William, who continued talking without her.

"Somewhere...in Pathia?" I started. "Okay, I don't know where exactly. But! The important thing is that we need to work together to find him."

"We're doing fine without him," William said.

"Are you? Really? You need his specialist knowledge to pull this off. Even if you were successful, you think that the entire country is just going to switch to a new economic system overnight?"

"There will be a period of transition," William said.

"Yeah, I've heard that before. I didn't think much of that plan, either."

"She's right." Eade sounded like the words were sour in her mouth. "We need to work together. Either you help us find Bombilate, or we can leave and do this on our own."

"What's your interest in him?" William asked.

"Eade worked with him," I said.

"Odd, he never mentioned you." William regarded Eade with a steady glare.

"He never mentioned you, either," she snapped back.

I started again, thinking about compromise. The best place to start would be getting them to agree on something. "Professor Bombilate is an intelligent man. We all agree on that." I waited while they nodded. "He is an instrument for change. Change can be good. If it's done right, it can be great."

"It can also be a disaster," Eade muttered.

"We can prevent a disaster, if we work together to find Professor Bombilate. Maybe he can help bring the Knotstick Order to justice for their use of empathic energy."

William shrugged, and even Eade looked less interested. At least that made two things they could agree on.

"What do we know about Professor Bombilate's disappearance?" I asked. The room went quiet, no one leapt to be the first to speak up.

"Who saw him last?"

"Technically, we all did," William replied. "At different times, I guess."

"So when did you last see Professor Bombilate?" I kept pushing to the point.

"Ahh… It would have been a month ago? He came to our committee meeting," William looked around and his comrades nodded in agreement.

"Did he seem distressed, concerned, afraid for his life?" I asked.

"No more than usual," William said.

"Professor Bombilate doesn't fear anything," Eade insisted.

"Except the complete collapse of civilisation as we know it," William replied.

"If he never feared anything and then suddenly threw in his lot with the Credit Union, as a revolutionary, then I would say he found out something that scared the doughnuts out of him."

No one laughed, which was my biggest fear. They all stared at the floor, then each other, and finally at me.

"The professor started working on something about four months ago," Eade said. "He didn't talk to me about the details, but I was used to that. He was always researching something."

"Did he leave any notes?"

Eade gave a sharp, hacking laugh. "As if he would write anything down. In Pathia you learn to keep things in your head. When the professor is ready, he types it all up and the information gets distributed through the various informercials."

It made a strange kind of sense. When knowledge is currency, writing stuff down would be like printing your own money. "Where does he do his thinking?" I asked.

"In his head," Eade replied, right on cue.

"Where does he go when he is thinking?" I tried again.

"His home office, usually," Eade replied.

"Doesn't he work with you in the museum?" I asked.

"Sometimes. He's usually out there talking to people, putting things together. Working out his ideas."

"People, ideas, observation. He sees things and makes connections," I summarised.

"We haven't found him, though," Eade reminded everyone.

"Because we haven't been looking. Not really looking." I felt a breakthrough coming up through my skin. A rippling wave of *ah-ha!* "We just need to go where he is, not where we think he should be."

"Genius," Eade said, with so much sarcasm she sounded like she was speaking a different dialect.

"It's like we can either know which direction he is going in, or where he is. But not both."

"This is a man, not a quantum probability," Eade replied.

"The principle is the same. We can find him if we know where he is."

"Okay, you're making no sense at all," Eade said, rolling her eyes.

"She's making perfect sense," Drakeforth spoke for the first time in half a chapter.

"Well by all means, illuminate the rest of us." Eade sat down and folded her arms.

"If we know where Professor Bombilate is, we will find him.

To know where he is, we have to know why he is there. The answer to that seems to be connected with the activities of the Credit Union, which recently gained the support of Bombilate and the Knotstick Order, which has a vested interest in keeping things exactly as they are. Which can best be described as complete cauliflowery obfuscation of their side operation in harvesting double-e flux and probably selling it to the Godden Energy Corporation."

William spoke up: "Which means they are already undermining the current system, and the only reason they would do that is because they know how unsustainable it is."

Goat woke up and sprang from the depths of the sofa with a wordless yell. He blinked and looked around in confusion.

"It's heavier than it looks," he said.

"Is he okay?" William asked.

"I think he suffers from heat stroke," Eade said. "Too much time out in the desert with no working air-con."

"If we are agreed that we need to find Professor Bombilate, then—" William started, when I interrupted him.

"We need to go." I turned in a full circle, looking for an exit.

"Where?" Eade asked.

"Wherever Pudding leads," Drakeforth replied. He stood up and put his hat on.

CHAPTER 39

The Credit Union filed out of the lounge and onto the stone floor where the van was parked. We piled in and waited while the warehouse door was cranked open. One of the Credit Union soldiers ducked under the narrow gap and then came scrambling back inside.

"Sandies!" he shouted, and ran towards the lounge. We watched as he scooped up the half-empty sandwich platters and ran into the deeper shadows of the warehouse.

"Police," Eade explained.

"Is there a back door out of here?" Drakeforth asked.

"Creditors," William ordered, "enact Plan Unicorn."

The van emptied even faster than it had been filled. People scattered in all directions, while we sat in confusion.

"I'll drive," Eade announced, and climbed into the front seat. She started the engine and stirred the gear stick until she found reverse. The van leapt backwards and skidded on the smooth floor. Eade worked the stick like a pilot in a flat spin stall. The van tyres spun and smoked. We gripped our seats as the van roared towards the exit. Police vehicles with flashing lights were converging in the street outside. Eade twisted the wheel and we shot through a narrow gap before hurtling down a street lined with matching industrial garage doors.

The rear window lit up with the insistent flashing lights of pursuing police. Eade ignored them and we slid sideways around a corner, straightened up and, in a remarkable act of coincidence, we merged with traffic on a busier street and everything settled into a strange sense of unusual calm.

"Where was it you wanted to go?" Eade asked.

"Ah, the museum?" I replied.

Eade hit the brakes and we head-banged like a mosh pit snap-shot.

She turned and frowned at me. "Why do you want to go there?"

"I have an idea," I said. "I want to go back to the museum to check something out."

Behind us, a loud honking sound erupted. I looked around, wondering what had happened.

"I'm not going anywhere until you tell me why," Eade warned.

"Eade! Drive the darraign car!" Drakeforth yelled. She scowled and hit the throttle. The van swerved through traffic and Eade hit the horn. Instead of the polite coughing of a regular car horn, a blasting howl roared at other cars, which answered with their own bullfrog mating calls. The noise was deafening.

"She's a better driver than you," I said to Drakeforth as we avoided death by the narrowest margin once again.

"Eade has a licence," Drakeforth replied.

"You don't have a licence?"

"Never got round to it."

Eade cut through a congested intersection like a pinch of pepper-snuff and stopped long enough to reverse us into an alley-way.

I waited for a second. "I know I've only been in Pathia for a few days, but I'm pretty sure this isn't the museum."

"Quiet." Eade's focus on the roadway was intense. We sat in a stuffy and rapidly warming silence until a squad of police cars shot past. Eade turned into traffic and we calmly went the other way.

CHAPTER 40

I got some sleep on the way to the museum—not helpful if I ever needed to find the place—which, for reasons I didn't consider a priority, seemed to be in the middle of the desert and far away from civilisation.

"Morning," Drakeforth said when I sat up.

"Urgh?" I asked.

"Almost lunch time," Drakeforth replied.

We climbed out of the van, which Eade had stopped in the carpark in the shadow of the museum building.

"Wish we had known this was here last time," I said. "Goat could have parked his airship and come with us."

"Of course trousers migrate," Goat said. "Why else would they have legs?"

"Staff entrance is this way," Eade said. We walked up a less intimidating stone staircase, and waited while Eade swiped an access card and unlocked the door.

The cool air washed over us and Goat backed up so fast he collided with Drakeforth.

"It's cool," Drakeforth said. "Nothing to worry about."

Goat nodded, his eyes sweeping around the corridor we found ourselves in.

"Reminds me of a joke," he said.

Eade flicked a switch and the hallway filled with light. We moved along in an orderly fashion.

"Is there a bathroom?" I asked Eade.

She nodded, "Yes. Yes, there is."

I clenched. "Good to know."

I saw the sign and turned off into a bathroom where the facilities were typically Pathian. If the currency revolution that the Credit Union wanted to bring about was successful, someone could make a fortune selling moisturiser.

The corridor was empty when I returned. I followed it through various rooms filled with stone shelves and metal boxes that looked like they contained papers and files. The Pathian equivalent of a bank vault. *Why does no one just break in and steal all this information?*

I kept walking, past shelves and through various rooms without labels or even numbers. I went down different corridors, turning in various directions with the same disconnected approach that had brought us here previously.

At the back of a broom closet, which turned out to be a very short corridor, I found a door that opened inwards. The other side was panelled wall, hiding the door from the other side.

The room was familiar: the rubble on the floor, the broken glass, and the murrai footprints in the dust.

I wandered through the shattered gallery until I found where the air-conditioning unit had stood. In its place was a sarcophagus, a carefully sculpted frieze of a human figure that, if it wasn't some kind of burial casket, would have made an amazing jelly mould.

I ran my hands over the case, which was cold to the touch and humming like a refrigerator. Maybe it was an air conditioner? I found the back edge and worked my fingers into the narrow gap against the wall. Leaning against the metal side, I tried to move it. *Where's a murrai when you need one?*

Something gave way and the cover slid forward. I scrambled to catch it before the entire shell crashed to the floor. It might be an ancient relic, for all I knew.

With the sarcophagus removed, I could get a closer look at the metal cylinder. It was less aesthetically pleasing than the last one I had seen. This one wasn't meant for public use. No one would go willingly into this. The sarcophagus disguise was apt.

The Godden Energy Corporation had shown me the double-e flux reclamation tank before I went into it. That one was nice:

warmly coloured and accessorised with the kind of useless bling usually found on the outside of coffins.

This looked like an industrial model. All practical function and no frivolity. I found the control panel and tapped at the soft keys until a menu came up on the screen.

I pressed the touchscreen "Status" option.

"Transfer Complete," the screen replied.

Frowning, I selected the command to open the tank. The machine clanked and gurgled. Then, with the hiss of a freshly opened carbonated beverage, the two halves of the pod separated.

I waved the mist aside and stared at the empty case where I'd been sure Professor Bombilate would be.

CHAPTER 41

"It's okay, I can hear a light," Goat said, and the three of them came through the broom closet and into the exhibit hall where I was sitting on a 4th Century shucking stool and frowning.

"He's not here," I announced.

"He's not?" Eade seemed genuinely surprised. She went to the double-e flux extractor and looked inside. "Where's he gone?"

"Everywhere," I said. "Wherever the Godden Energy Corporation has a need for power, he will be there. He'll be running toasters, empathically empowered cars, street lights, computers, and hot water systems."

"You knew he was here," Drakeforth said.

I blinked; he'd said it. He didn't ask.

"You knew...?" Clarity hit me like the first wave on a midwinter swim. "You knew!? You knew the whole time that he was in here and you let us do *what*? Run around the desert and nearly get killed and actually get arrested and you knew he was here the entire time?"

"I can explain," Eade replied. She moved fast for an archaeologist; all that time spent crouched in the dirt must give them steel springs for thighs. She was through the broom closet door and pulling it shut before I could finish drawing breath to shout a warning.

The wall closed seamlessly, and I pounded on it while imagining it was Eade's face.

"Drakeforth, you'd be okay with me burying Eade up to her neck in an ant nest, wouldn't you?"

"I'll bring the shovels," he replied.

"There's no harm in trying," Goat said.

"No harm at all," I nodded. "We should get to the car park before she escapes."

"Then what?" Drakeforth asked. "Aside from burying her up to the neck in an ant nest. We have lost Professor Bombilate. Really lost him, we should just go home and pretend none of this ever happened."

"No," I said. "I'm not letting the Godden Energy Corporation, Eade Notschnott, and the Knotstick Order get away with mass murder again."

"Excellent. How, exactly?" Drakeforth asked.

"The Credit Union," I replied.

"They have some interesting ideas that will not amount to as much change as they think. Consider what they really want. It's not revolution, but a share of the profits. They don't give a fig's fingernail about where the money is coming from. The Credit Union only want to get their hands on as much of it as possible."

"Nothing changes," I said. "Religion or corporate greed, it's all about money and the people are always going to get scoured."

"The real question is, are we going to stop them, and if so, how?"

"We need a revolution of our own," I replied. Then I thought about it. "Actually, that's exactly what we need. A proper revolution, not just a reshuffle of the economic system."

"What did you have in mind?" Drakeforth raised an eyebrow. "Burning this place down?"

I gasped in horror, "Gazebos no! This museum is full of priceless artefacts. This is history, people have worked tirelessly for generations to carefully restore and identify every item here. I would no more burn a place like this down than I would, well, burn down a museum."

"Okay, arson is out." Drakeforth looked disappointed.

"What if we devalued information to the point where the truth becomes meaningless?"

"You want to start a conservative news network?"

I shook my head. "That would take too long. We need to get

information to the people, like, litter the streets with answers to questions people never knew they had."

"Do you know why it is illegal to drop litter in Pathia, Pudding?"

"There's more to it than cultural pride and concerted effort to keep the environment free of pollution?"

"They burn fossil fuel, which creates more pollution than any other source. The reason is that it keeps the information in the hands of those who benefit from it. If you hang on to every scrap of paper, every note, every piece of packaging you acquire, you will value it. It's one of the driving principles of their economic success."

"We're going to have to break the law for this to work," I said.

"To do that, we need some information that no one else has and that people will want to acquire."

"Okay, what about Professor Bombilate's latest research? He clearly worked out that it's all unsustainable. Now we have to tell everyone."

"Pathians don't tend to write things down unless it's garment washing instructions," Drakeforth said.

"Maybe he had something. Notes, or diagrams, or raw data?"

"It's where the term *money laundering* comes from," Drakeforth continued.

"He has an office here somewhere." I walked around the exhibit hall. Finding another way into the back corridors without a staff swipe card would be tricky.

"Goat, do you know anything about opening locked doors?"

"Key?" Goat replied.

"Well yes, but without a key?"

Goat fell into step beside me, "Easier if the door isn't locked."

"At home, I could try communicating with the empathic energy in the security system and see if I could ask it nicely to open…" I stopped suddenly and Goat walked into me.

"Sorry," I said and, Goat nodded furiously at the floor. "Drakeforth, what is an informercial?"

"It's like an ATM machine, used to distribute information to those who have sufficient credit to make a withdrawal."

"Eade said that Professor Bombilate's research would be distributed through the usual informercials."

"It makes sense."

"Can we access that from any computer terminal?"

"Any terminal connected to the net," Drakeforth replied.

"Great, now we just need to find a network terminal."

"What's a horse?" Goat asked.

"Goat appears to have found a way in," Drakeforth said.

"What? That's great. How?" I asked as I went to where Goat stood next to an open door.

Goat looked sideways,

"Good work." I stepped past him and into an office. There were several computers here, brand new Celerytron model desktops. I slipped into a seat in front of one and powered it up.

The login screen came up and I took a chance. User name: *User1* Password: *Password1*. The computer thought about it for a moment and then flashed up a home screen.

"I turned the handle and it opened," Goat announced.

"These computers haven't been used before. They're new installations. No specific user accounts have been set up, so the default account names and passwords are still valid."

"How does that help us?" Drakeforth gently pushed Goat to one side and came into the office.

"Well, it means we have administrator access to the entire network. However this was set up, we can get in and poke about."

"I've never really got on well with computers," Drakeforth said.

"A lot of people find technology intimidating," I said in my best new user customer support advisor voice.

"I don't find it intimidating," Drakeforth replied. "The last time I used a computer, it came up with an error message something like, *User error. Replace user and press any key to continue.*"

"Empathically powered machines respond best to a calm and measured approach. It's like riding a horse—"

"Something best avoided at all costs," Drakeforth interrupted.

"And much like riding a horse, you need to have a firm hand, and a calm demeanour."

"Why am I riding this horse?" Drakeforth asked.

"The horse is a metaphor. You don't need to have a reason to be riding the horse."

"Great, I'd like to get off."

"This stuff would make great sailcloth," Goat said.

"Forget the horse. We approach the computer calmly and with confidence." I tapped some keys and brought up the browser window. I typed *Informercials* into the search window. The system thought for a moment and then showed me what I wanted. Lots and lots of technical data, all streaming across the screen.

"Tree..." Goat whispered.

"Tree," I agreed. My fingers flew across the keyboard as my eyes picked out the relevant lines of code. I cut, edited, and interrupted processes, creating a software bot that would operate as a sleek data-seeking torpedo. It was a basic construct with a simple instruction: go out into the dark ocean of the net and find anything with Professor Bombilate's data signature on it.

"How long is this going to take?" Drakeforth asked.

"I have no idea," I replied.

"I only ask because my horse is getting tired."

"Maybe you should get off and let the horse ride for a while?"

"I was going to offer, but it didn't seem in keeping with the firm hand approach."

The torpedo came back and regurgitated information onto the screen. I stared at it: many references to published papers and offshore news articles. I filtered the results based on Pathian informercial hits. There were three within the last month.

"Okay, I have found something. One transmittal came from here. It's a pre-load of data, not the final report. They get the data but the key to decrypt it is withheld."

"Everything has its price," Drakeforth said.

"One of the others came from..." Cross-referencing the terminal source address with the physical address was a simple search, but it looked good to anyone who knew nothing about computers. "There."

"That's in the city," Drakeforth read off the screen. "What about the third transfer?"

"No actual address, a mobile connection. Which came from somewhere near the city, but out in the desert."

"Errm," Drakeforth said immediately. "The third transfer was from the dig site in the ruins of Errm."

"I can't actually see what was uploaded, not without the encryption key," I said.

"We go there," Drakeforth replied. "Errm, and that address in the city."

"It's a long walk, or we can call a litter," I said.

"Make it a litter for three."

CHAPTER 42

The ruins of Errm were still a hive of activity. Trenches cut into the layers of sand while workers swarmed in the dust, extracting the fragments of the past like there was no future.

A familiar figure with black hair flitted between the tents and tables in parallel to us as we crossed the dig site. I focused on not paying her any attention. Her presence was a hallucination that I had little time for.

Equally familiar, but far more welcome, was the tent where Geddon Withitt had passed away. Goat and I stood nonchalantly while shielding Drakeforth from view as he untied the door flap.

We slipped through the gap and once the four of us were stuffed inside, the interior was darker and hotter than inside a cooked chicken.

"There should be a net terminal here somewhere," I said edging forward and blinking in the gloom.

"It'll be small, like a phone or a tablet."

"I always found the idea of tablets a hard pill to swallow," Drakeforth said.

I frowned at him. "Why is it every time we are here, you start with the stupid jokes?"

"In spite of appearances, I don't like being around dead people or places where they recently died."

"I've seen more dead people since I met you than I have in my entire life. I've been almost killed more times, too."

Drakeforth found the one sliver of daylight and stood in its glow. "Are you saying that is my fault?"

"Of course it is your fault. None of this would have happened if you hadn't dragged me along on this cabrilla of an adventure."

"Pudding, you must realise now that none of this is my doing. You are acting entirely on the initiative of your own fate. All of this—the Godden Energy Corporation, the Arthurians, the running from certain death towards high-probability of maiming and permanent mental trauma—all you."

While I feel grief, misery, pain, and screaming frustration regularly, crying isn't something I do often. I swallowed the sensation of my eyeballs swelling with tears, and was glad for the deep shadows that hid the shine.

"I'm dying, Drakeforth."

"We're all dying," he replied.

"Yes, but listen. I'm really dying. You probably haven't had a chance to read the manuscript I left in the Living Oak desk, but—"

"I saw it. It was with your note."

"It's a strange disease. Nothing as cliché as cancer or a rampant fungal infection. My doctor did a lot of tests, which I gather I failed. Which is annoying; I have always been good at tests. I can expect a gradual decline in physical and neurological function, he said. Symptoms include tiredness and non-specific pain. Yes, my doctor diagnosed me with modern living."

"What are your treatment options?"

"Nothing that will cure it. Just palliative care."

"Which is why you went to GEC and did the deal to have your double-e flux extracted in one mass?"

"They were going to put me in the Python Building, to replace my grandfather in the failing engine."

"You would have been miserable there," Drakeforth said.

"I'm not sure I would have been anything. I mean, my consciousness would have gone but I would have been useful, you know?"

"If I knew this was going to be a pity-party, I would have brought cake and balloons," Drakeforth replied.

I managed a smile, "Sure. A sendoff like that would have been worth staying alive for."

"I'll check Withitt's desk." Drakeforth slipped from light to dark and filled a silhouette behind the desk.

Drawers rattled and opened. Goat was running his fingertips along the canvas sheets of the tent and seemed to approve of the cloth. "We're going to need more goats," he muttered to himself.

"This looks promising," Drakeforth announced. He tapped a desk lamp and the tent filled with the light of the sun on a heavily overcast day. Drakeforth laid a mobile tablet on the desk and regarded it with the disdain normally reserved for well-hung roadkill.

"Let's have a look." I took the tablet and frowned at the requirement for a password, or a retina scan or a recorded fingerprint.

"Shame Withitt isn't still here," I said.

"You think she would be more cooperative this time around?" Drakeforth asked.

"No, but we could use her finger to unlock this device."

"If it has an empathic battery, could you maybe talk nicely to it?"

I snorted and was going to say something sarcastic, when it occurred to me that he might be right. With one hand on the screen, I closed my eyes and thought gentle, warm thoughts at the device under my touch.

The tablet whispered and warmed, I felt the swirl of empathic energy tingling my skin until it left a message at the beep.

It was there: the encrypted file in the sent folder of his mail app. "Hello, Professor Bombilate," I murmured.

"The doctor is in?" Drakeforth asked.

"Professor, the professor is in," I corrected. "Now, we have to find the rest of the information. It will be enough to shake things up and if we can work out the key to decrypt the files, we can *really* shake things up."

"We need to do more than shake things up, we need to break things down."

"Revealing the truth about the Godden Energy Corporation didn't change anything," I reminded him.

"These are different people, they have a long history of upheaval and change. Conflict and revolution has been a national sport in Pathia for centuries. These people love nothing more than starting a fight over a new idea."

"If we give them enough information, they can do what they want with it. If that means societal change, then great. If it means everyone just shrugs and goes on with their lives, then not so great, but okay."

"Life would be so much simpler without people," Drakeforth replied.

"Let's get out of here before someone comes and asks stupid questions." I tucked the tablet into my coat and pulled my hat down over my eyes.

Goat gave the canvas wall one final caress and followed us out of the tent.

Our litter bearers reclined in the shade of their carriers as we casually strolled through the dig site towards them.

"Don't look to your right," Drakeforth warned.

Of course I glanced in that direction immediately. Nothing out of the ordinary, so I looked the other way and saw Eade in fervent conversation with the clipboard carrier.

"*Sheep!*" I muttered. "Do you think she saw us?"

"It's not her I'm worried about, so much as them," Drakeforth replied.

"Who are they?" I squinted in the glare and tried to make out the details of the figures shimmering in the heat haze.

"Knotstick Order," Drakeforth replied. "Here to keep everything under the control of the grand Sybil."

"Those sibilus things are whistles for murrai. If we get one of those whistles, we might be able to create a distraction."

"Shame they don't sell them in the gift shop," Drakeforth said.

"There's no gift shop here, but…"

"You think you can teach an old stone new tricks?" Drakeforth asked. I turned on my heel and marched back into the dusty maelstrom.

Finding an abandoned clipboard was easy. I held it like a shield against questions, and moved along the tables of artefacts waiting to be sorted and categorised. Shards of pottery, dirt-encrusted coins, and the occasional stone tablet were on display. I stopped at a box of possible candidates. A young man with his hair tied back was carefully brushing caked sand off some kind of stone whisk.

I rummaged through the box and found a dark stone whistle, like the one Nonce wore around his neck. I glanced up and the whisk brusher was watching me. "What is this doing in here?" I snapped.

"Its uh—"

"It's clearly Copra Dynasty, and the rest of these items are Cobra Dynasty. Mixing them up could get you fired."

"I didn't—"

"Oh, forget it. I'll take care of it. Just don't mention your incompetence to anyone else."

"Uhh, thank you," he managed.

I walked off, quietly pleased that I had gotten away with it.

"Hey!" someone shouted. I kept walking. "You! In the hat!" I walked faster; there were a lot of people in hats. It was the desert; not wearing something on your head was a good way to get your brain steamed.

The slap of running feet on sand came closer. I ducked under a rope and tried to ignore the subtle, panicked gestures Drakeforth was making at me.

Goat sprang forward, twisted past me with the grace and agility of someone who'd spent a lot of time balancing on ropes, and spread his arms.

"Goose! Goose!" he yelled, and ran flapping at the knot of workers who were in pursuit.

I looked back. The workers were stumbling to a halt and clustering together as Goat descended on them. While I had never herded anything myself, the principle seemed straightforward, and Goat had an apparent knack for it.

Drakeforth was watching the proceedings with his usual razor-focused contempt.

"I got it," I whispered.

"Great, now play a tune or whatever it does and see what happens."

I put the sibilus to my lips and blew in it. A puff of dust shot out of a hole in the end. I blew it again. No sound, but I felt the blast ripple out and echo off the stonework.

Four murrai jerked up from their labours and turned to face me across the dig site. The people around them backed away as the stone men began to march. The volume of shouts rose as they stepped over and around the work underway in their shadows.

Eade looked around and saw us. Drakeforth waved. She waved back with one finger. I blew on the silent whistle and the murrai picked up their pace. Falling into line, the four of them came straight towards us.

Goat continued running around the workers he had corralled, and then veered off to chase the murrai.

Blowing the whistle was like yelling for attention, it seemed. The detailed instructions were transmitted in the intent. Like when I was driving the murrai across the desert. I waved at them and indicated where they should stop.

"Climb up," I said, and we scrambled onto the shoulders of giants.

CHAPTER 43

Riding a murrai might be like riding a bike, but at least it wasn't something I was going to forget in a hurry.

With legs locked around the statue's shoulders, I tried to move with its rocking gait. Goat was showing off by standing on his, one foot on its flat-top head, the other on the shoulder as casually as he might stand on the deck of his ship.

Drakeforth could have been riding in a litter for all the attention he gave. He stared back at the vanishing dig site. I hoped Eade was having trouble getting to her transport and following us.

I made semaphore hand signals, directing traffic and feeling relieved that the murrai were still accepting my advice on navigation.

As captains of our two-legged ships, we crested dunes until the regular motion started making me feel sick. I watched the horizon and thought about the various types of ice-cold tea I was going to devote my life to sampling once we returned to the world.

The long sunset turned the shadows to fire and smoke. The sand reflected a thousand colours, and shards of light danced in every grain. At this time of day, the desert could be a landscape of double-e flux, the sparks of life scattered by the seven winds. Each tiny part ground down from the rock of a person, an existence that was as complete and inviolate as a mountain.

Semita's lights brought us into land like the runway of a zippelin port. Our mounts strode from sand to smooth rock and on to the pyramid paving of the city streets. The people we passed barely glanced at the murrai, until they saw us on their shoulders. Then they stared and nudged their companions to look and see.

Our small parade marched on until we paused so I could ask directions. Following the advice given, we walked up a street lined with cars and carefully-tended dead trees. Professor Bombilate lived in a yellowstone townhouse with steps leading up to a stone door painted in a pale blue that matched the window trims.

We parked and climbed down. "Uhm...*stay*," I ordered the murrai. They didn't move when we climbed the steps and I hoped they would be there when we came out.

"Should we knock?" I asked. Drakeforth raised a hand and then dropped it again. The door opened and I opened my mouth to explain why we were on their doorstep.

The pale woman leaned back against the wall, merging with the darkness so only the whites of her eyes and the pale milk of her skin stood out.

"The door seems to be already open," Drakeforth said, and stepped inside.

At university, I never went into a professor's apartment, townhouse or bathroom. I saw plenty of their offices, always stacked high with books and papers. The impression was always that they were just ahead of us on the learning curve and were desperate to keep ahead by cramming as much knowledge as possible into their own heads before giving us stuff we could have worked out for ourselves with a few pointers and a library card.

By contrast, Professor Bombilate's house was empty of everything but furniture. It could have been a show-home for a real estate developer, except for the dishes in the drying rack and the pile of single socks on the kitchen table.

"Split up, search the place, meet at the socks in ten minutes," Drakeforth said.

We went in different directions, leaving Goat turning in circles in the living room. I headed upstairs. Bathroom, bedrooms...one appeared to be used regularly, the other a pristine guest room.

I went back out into the hallway, noted the bathroom, bedrooms, and went around them again. I stepped into the bathroom, back into the hall, counting my steps as I went into the guest room. There was a sense of façade about the place. I tapped a wall. It sounded solid enough. I tapped other walls in other rooms, each sounding as sound as you would expect.

Inside the closet of the main bedroom were identical suits, freshly dry, dusted and pressed. I slid the clothes along the rail and pressed the panels on the back wall. Something clicked and a section popped out. I pulled the small door open and went to find Drakeforth.

"Guys, there's a secret panel in the—" I went silent as I noticed the extra people standing in the living room. Drakeforth was on the sofa, while Goat lay stretched out on the floor with two men holding him down.

"Miss Pudding," Nonce said, appearing from the kitchen. "So nice to meet you again."

"I'd rather see my dentist," I replied. "What are you doing here, Mister Nonsense?"

"Grand Linteum Nonce," he corrected. "I am the current head of the Knotstick Order."

"I'm a lifetime member of the Cragmark fan club," I replied.

"Miss Pudding, we both know why we are here. May I suggest you hand over anything you have regarding the late Professor Bombilate and we will be on our way."

"I told you, we don't have anything," Drakeforth said from the couch. One of Nonce's priests flexed his knuckles behind Drakeforth's head.

"I have faith in you," Nonce said. "We know you were at the dig site at Errm. You left rather quickly, and, might I add, in an unusual manner."

"Doesn't everyone travel by murrai?" I asked with wide-eyed innocence.

"There aren't many of the machines left. It's not common to see someone control them as adeptly as you clearly do."

"It's simply a case of purse your lips and blow," I replied.

"I have no time for word games," Nonce said, his smile frosting over.

"Who's playing?" I replied, my eyes locked on his.

"I'm keeping score, if that helps," Drakeforth said from the sidelines.

A priest with banana-sized fingers that were in perfect proportion to the rest of him, stepped forward. "We will take what you have," he growled.

"Fine." I slipped a hand into my pocket and blew the murrai whistle before they could grab me. The front door exploded inwards, most of the hallway and tasteful furniture flew into the kitchen. The men of the Knotstick Order ducked for cover as the murrai walked through into the living room as if the walls were paper.

"I hope you found what we needed," Drakeforth shouted over the noise of the house demolition.

"Not quite. Upstairs, quick!" We ducked under a swinging murrai fist and Goat crawled under the rug and wore it like a shell as he scuttled after us.

Grand Linteum Nonce was blowing his murrai whistle until his cheeks bulged. The murrai ignored his commands and I could feel them drawing on my own panicked energy. We ran up the stairs and into Bombilate's bedroom. I threw the closet door open and indicated the open panel. Drakeforth reached in and grabbed the carefully wrapped box hidden in the secret alcove.

He handed it to me and then checked to see if we had missed anything. "That's everything, unless you want to try a suit?" Drakeforth asked.

"I'm good."

The stairs collapsed as two Knotstick priests tried to hold back a murrain, and the stone man did a stumbling pirouette. Goat knotted the end of the rug around his neck and wore it like a cloak.

Drakeforth threw the curtains open and slid the window along its track. "Pudding, do you think you could bring our ride around the back?"

"I miss that car," I replied. With a shift in focus, a murrai went through the kitchen wall under our feet and emerged in the back rock garden.

"Now we jump?" Drakeforth asked.

"Genome!" Goat yelled, and took a running jump through the open window. The murrai caught him and set him down on the warm sand.

I climbed out and jumped, remembering to breathe only when I was placed next to Goat. Drakeforth stepped out as casually as a man leaving a house the usual way. He set foot on the murrai's sandstone palm and stepped down.

"Send the murrai somewhere, we will go the other way," Drakeforth ordered. I nodded; it made sense. Even though the idea of three rock star bodyguards was very enticing.

The murrai gatecrashed on the way out, much the way they came in. We scrambled over the back wall and across the neighbour's yard as Professor Bombilate's house collapsed behind us.

"Well, that's one way to cover our tracks," I said.

We flagged down a litter and the three of us crammed inside while the carriers bent their knees and lifted us to their shoulders.

"Are you going to open it?" Drakeforth asked.

"Sure, I guess. Okay." The box was tied shut with twine, and I frowned at the knots but Goat took the package from me and gnawed on the string until it snapped.

"Thanks." I took the box back and opened it. Inside was a Celerytron notebook and a carefully wrapped soft package that I hoped would be the missing shroud.

CHAPTER 44

The Hotel Dust had a comforting familiarity, and the woman (I stared at her until I was certain) behind the reception desk barely glanced in our direction as we crossed the lobby.

Drakeforth opened the door to our room and we set the box down on the bed.

"Goat, you should take a shower." I pointed towards the bathroom door.

Goat indicated the door and raised an eyebrow. I nodded and waved him in that direction. He opened the door, peered inside, and looked back at me with a question writ large on his face.

"Yes, *shower*. Come back when you and your…clothes are clean."

When he had gone, Drakeforth handed me the computer out of the box. "This is for you. I'll have a look at the sheet."

Celerytron computers use empathically empowered technology. That meant the new desktop PCs at the museum, and this notebook, were recently imported.

I stared at the screen as the machine booted up. The familiar GEC heart and lightning bolt logo glowing in high-definition.

"Godden Energy Corporation provided the technology to the Knotstick Order. New computers and a whole lot of information in return for the steady supply of double-e flux."

"Where does Professor Bombilate fit in to all of this?" Drakeforth asked.

"Currently, he probably fits between half a dozen cities and innumerable home appliances. Prior to his being converted to double-e flux, he was the man holding it all together."

"An idea is a fragile thing," Drakeforth said. "Bombilate nurtured the idea of an idea. He gave it to the Pathians and they ran with it. He made something as perfect and delicate as a soap bubble. This—" He carefully unfolded the shroud, "—is an original idea. A moment in time, preserved forever. The perfect distillation of a thought."

"It's lines and circles and some kind of numbers?" I peered at the sheet.

"Arthur's first revelation. He never intended it as the foundation of an entire religion. He just thought many thoughts that were too big and exciting for him to contain."

"He sounds like an interesting person," I said.

"Arthur was just a man. No smarter or more socially adept than the rest of us. He made cringe-worthy mistakes and some remarkable leaps of logic. If he hadn't recorded the core principles of his theory of relatives on this linen sheet, he would have been as forgotten as a thousand other prophets who lived at the same time."

"Strange how things work out," I said, my eyes still fixed on the most valuable religious artefact in the world.

"It's only strange when they work out. Can you log in to that?" Drakeforth asked.

"It's not the default user name and password. This system has been used and carefully configured." I rested my fingertips on the keyboard, feeling the hum of empathic energy glowing in the circuit boards and memory chips.

After a minute, Drakeforth cleared his throat.

"Something you need?" I asked, without opening my eyes.

"Access to this computer?" Drakeforth said.

I flexed my fingers and sat back. "You're welcome to try it yourself."

"User name, Bombilate?"

I keyed it in. "Now the password?"

Drakeforth thought for a moment. "We are talking about a very clever man. His password could be long and complex, or it could be as simple as Bombilate."

"Right," I smirked, and typed Bombilate into the password field and pressed *Enter*. The computer whirred and the login screen cleared.

"What happened?" Drakeforth asked.

"We logged in," I said, swallowing my astonishment.

Drakeforth shrugged as if it were nothing, and went back to studying the Shroud of Tureen. I found the encrypted file and transferred the other section from the tablet to the notebook.

The two pieces fit together like the world's simplest jigsaw puzzle, except it was still encrypted with a specific code key. I sighed and typed in *Bombilate*. The computer didn't quite laugh at me, but I felt like it should.

"What would Professor Bombilate use as an encryption key…?"

"Have you tried using his name, but with a zero and a one instead of the 'o' and the 'i'?" Drakeforth asked. He was on his hands and knees, his nose almost touching the grey fabric of the shroud.

"An encryption key needs to be something impossible to guess, but easy to remember. It's like any code: once you know the key, you can unlock the entire message."

"What would be the hardest thing to ever guess?" Drakeforth murmured his attention clearly on the sheet.

"A random sequence of numbers and letters," I replied.

"Arthur's formulae is the basis of some key concepts of quantum physics. Most of the work was done by more secular minds after his death, but he got people talking and thinking and, most importantly, doing some serious math."

"I'm not sure even a mathematician could crack this," I said.

"Arthur's Theory of Relatives came about because he realised that nothing exists unless it is perceived. He had a friend, a woman named Magnesia. She didn't know if her mother was alive or dead. Arthur concluded that she was neither alive nor dead, as long as Magnesia didn't know."

"That would have been weird for anyone who actually met the poor woman," I said.

"Arthur understood that probability meant she could be both;

in the Universe that Magnesia occupied, her mother could live forever, provided her daughter's perception was never altered to create a reality where she had deceased."

"Which helps us with the encryption key how, exactly?" I waited with my hands hovering over the keyboard. The answer felt close, and I itched to type it in.

"The key both exists and doesn't exist. It is in a state of flux. Until it is observed, it can be both up and down. Left and right, porcine and equine."

I inhaled and exhaled slowly. "The secret is to accept that you cannot know the key without destroying it."

"It's a start," Drakeforth agreed.

"It sure is…" I pressed the *Enter* key and the file started to unpack into a readable format.

While the secret Professor Bombilate had died for unpacked itself, Drakeforth found a way to secure the ancient Shroud of Tureen to the hotel room wall. We stood together, studying the faded marks and lines. Over the centuries, lines had formed along the fold marks. The meaning of the symbols lost in the creases had caused more deaths and claims of heresy than any other aspect of Arthurianism.

"You could solve a lot of arguments by simply telling people what it actually says," I said.

"I wrote it down with the expectation that people would accept the truth and it wouldn't be open to interpretation."

"People never accept anything, and everything is open to interpretation," I replied.

"You can see why I find them all so annoying."

"It's understandable," I agreed.

The bathroom door opened and a cloud of dust wafted out. A man walked into the room carrying an armload of cologne scent on his skin.

"Goat…?" I stared.

"Goat," he agreed. His eyes were furtive, skipping over the floor and the walls before landing on the Shroud of Tureen hanging from the wall.

"Tree…" he whispered.

"Shroud," I corrected automatically. "Goat, you look different."

The calcified lump of facial hair had been scraped off his face, his hair was clean, trimmed, and combed back. He had a deep tan and wore a towel.

"Tree…" Goat came closer, the towel forgotten as he reached out and almost touched the sheet.

"I should find him some pants," Drakeforth said. He went to his suitcase and retrieved clothes for Goat.

The notebook beeped, confirming that the file reconstruction was complete. I went to the computer and started reading. In the background, Drakeforth struggled to get Goat dressed.

CHAPTER 45

"'And in conclusion'," I read aloud, "'it is my belief that the future of Pathia as a stable and sovereign nation requires that we take all necessary steps to ensure the integration of a modern and robust credit unit system which will allow us to compete on international markets and increase the stability and productivity of our domestic industries.' Yeah, he goes on like this for…another three pages."

"That's quite the revelation," Drakeforth said.

"Faith in the economy is what keeps the economy growing. Bombilate said it, and the Knotsticks are losing their sand over it. If people question their faith in the current standard value of the knowledge economy, it will all fall apart."

"It will all fall apart eventually," Drakeforth replied. "It's not faith in knowledge that keeps the Pathian economy turning the pages of the ledgers. The faith people have in the artefacts and ideals on display in places like the museum is what drives economic growth."

Drakeforth sipped a cup of tea. "In Pathia, the Godden Energy Corporation doesn't need to harvest double-e flux from the dying. They are gathering it from the faith inherent in the system. The knowledge economy and the careful regulation of that knowledge."

"Well yes, Bombilate goes into detail about that in his research paper. That's why they killed him. He was going to destabilise everything. The dig at Errm: the Knotsticks are looking for new artefacts to inspire faith."

"Strong faith will protect the markets against the revolution that is to come," Drakeforth nodded.

"Tree," Goat said.

"Right, so where is the technology they are using to extract all this latent empathic energy?"

"In the pyramids," Drakeforth said.

"Tree," Goat said.

"That's where they are storing it. The Godden engine we saw was simply a pump, keeping everything ticking over. We've seen no evidence of a pipe or cable network in the desert."

"Same as their internet service, radio waves and satellite."

"Tree," Goat said.

I shook my head. "Empathic energy doesn't travel wirelessly. Outside of the range of an empowered object's anthropomorphic field, the radiance dissipates. It has to be sent through some kind of pipe or cabling system."

We fell silent, both lost in thought.

"Boat," Goat announced, and stood up. "Ah, Tree. Tea. Boat. You're welcome, it's what I was trying to tell you earlier. If we are going to save the world, then we should get to the roof *immmm*— no, not yet. Wait. Here." He gestured for us to both remain where we were, and backed towards the door. A moment later, he was gone.

"We should follow him," I said.

Drakeforth stood up and collected his hat.

Goat was halfway down the stairs when we caught up with him. He nodded in acknowledgement of us and bounded down the remaining flights and out into the street.

Once there he turned this way and that, agitation tightening his face.

"Goat, where are we going?"

"Sand. Ship. Tree," Goat pointed in three different directions, and seemed at a loss as to which way to go first.

"Where's the airship?" I asked.

"The police have it." Drakeforth joined Goat in the dance of uncertainty. "They'll have it in impound."

"Where is that?" I stepped in time with the other two.

"In Pathia," Drakeforth stopped dead.

"You think?" I glared.

"Yes, constantly, and even yet, I still manage to miss the occasional important detail. We need Harenae."

Finding a pathologist was a mysterious process that happened very quickly. We asked around and word spread, and the young woman with a map of the entire city in her head came strolling towards us within the hour. We had time to drink water and watch a funeral procession for a fly before she arrived. The mourners carried a platform with a tiny casket draped in flower petals. It was a solemn affair, and I wondered how the poor thing came to its end. At the end of the line, the woman in black twirled and danced. The floating material of her dress moved to its own current and she barely touched the ground. It seemed strange to celebrate death in this way, though the sorrow of the mourners was expressed in her every leap.

"Where to?" Harenae asked.

"Police impound lot. We need to collect our friend's...ahh... vehicle," I said.

"Easy," Harenae said. "Just the three of you? Any luggage this time?"

"No, just us."

"Walk this way," Harenae replied, and led us into a maze of narrow streets and alleyways. These were the places even litters couldn't fit, and we marched in single file under dusty awnings and past stalls selling spices and fruits that I couldn't name.

The police impound lot was mostly empty, and Goat's airship was tied down with more ropes than a circus tent.

Harenae led us to the kiosk and waited while we tried to explain the situation.

"Do you have your licence and registration?" the officer asked.

"Goat," Goat said.

"Yes, Mister Goat, however without documentation confirming your legal right to own and operate this vehicle of yours, we can't release it to you."

"Goat," Goat said.

"Do you think this officer knows how to spell pedestrian?" I murmured to Drakeforth.

Harenae shrugged off the shady wall she was leaning against, "Hey, Cuz."

The officer in the kiosk looked up and nodded, "Hey Hare, 'sup?"

"Not much. How's aunty?" Harenae asked.

"Sweet as," the officer replied. His dialect had gone from being relatively formal to back-dunes colloquial.

Harenae nodded and we stood in silence for a few moments. "Y'reckon y'can sort these pasties so I can get paid and get outta y'hair?"

"Yeah, nah," the officer scratched his jaw apologetically.

"Aww c'mon," Harenae grinned at him.

"Y'gonna get me in the fa'asi," he replied.

"Yeah, nah," Harenae grinned wider.

The officer sighed and slid off his chair. Exiting the kiosk, he came around and unlocked the gate to let us into the yard.

"Chur, bro," Harenae said.

"Come on, Goat. Let's get you in the air." I hurried him across the dusty ground to the tethered airship. Drakeforth signed forms for the officer and we untied the boat.

Goat scrambled aboard, and from the bleats of his herd, the crew were pleased to see their captain back on deck.

"Where you fellas goin'?" Harenae asked me.

"Where are we going?"

"Yeah—yes. Sorry, where are you planning on going in this?" Harenae switched to talking more like a woman with one of those private academy educations.

I hesitated, "Goat seems to have an idea on how the Knotstick Order are transferring the empathic energy they have been harvesting from the faith of those who believe in everything, from the knowledge economy to the sanctity of the Shroud of Tureen, to where they are storing it for the Godden Energy Corporation in reservoirs hidden inside the pyramids."

"You're looking for the path," Harenae replied.

"I don't know what we are looking for."

"Pathologists know the path. Sometimes the path isn't clear. But we know the path."

"You're pitching for more work?"

"I'm offering to help."

Drakeforth strode past us and climbed on to the boat as it started to strain against the last rope.

"Untie that last rope and jump on." I turned and scrambled over the rail.

"She's coming with us?" Drakeforth asked.

"Yeah."

"Good."

CHAPTER 46

The airship creaked and squeaked as it rose into the air. Goat was hard at work inflating additional intestines, using a strange contraption that seemed to work by siphoning gases from a tank of carefully collected goat waste, and pumping it into a narrow nozzle. With the casual ease of a clown at a child's birthday party, Goat tied off sausage balloons as they swelled with methane. The heat of the day expanded them further and the gas carried us higher.

We floated over a sprawling city that looked as insane as the paving that lined so many of its streets. Harenae stood at the bow and stared into the horizon.

Goat was at the wheel, which still didn't seem to be connected to anything functional. Perhaps it grounded him and gave a sense of stability. I wished I had something as simple as a wheel to hold onto.

"Hey," Harenae called from the rail. "there's someone following us."

I hurried over and looked where she pointed. A truck was hurtling through the narrow streets, scattering people and litters as it went. A lone figure stood in the open roof, a harpoon-like weapon cradled against their shoulder.

"What the harpsichord is that?" I asked.

"Serious intent?" the pathologist replied.

Smoke puffed from the rear of the weapon and a metal spear came rocketing towards us. We both ducked and the point buried itself in the goat balloon netting overhead. A rope went taut and we peered over the side again.

Eade Notschnott climbed the knotted rope with the determination of a caterpillar climbing towards the last leaf on a bush.

Drakeforth came over and looked down.

"You know how you had her declared legally dead?" I said. "I bet you regret not making sure first."

Drakeforth grunted and reached down to offer Eade a hand as she came into range. "Eade, how unpleasant of you to drop in unannounced."

"Vole, you need to stop. Just leave Pathia and stop."

"Stop what?" Drakeforth had an air of innocence about him that could have been sprayed from an aerosol can.

"Grand Linteum Nonce told me to get you here. I didn't know why at the time. I think it was because the Godden Energy Corporation wanted you taken care of."

"How generous of them," I said coldly.

"And quite unnecessary," Drakeforth replied. "I am reasonably adept at taking care of myself."

"They really don't like you," Eade insisted.

"No one likes Drakeforth," I said. "It's part of his charm."

"They were going to put you in the same cabinet as Professor Bombilate," Eade said.

"And you were okay with that?" I asked.

Eade paused for a moment. "I need to protect what I believe in. The museum, the artefacts, all that knowledge. It's real to me. Knowledge has value beyond the perceived worth of currency. You are putting all my work, my life's work at risk."

"You harpooned us to get that off your chest?" I asked.

"No, I harpooned you to stop you floating off into the desert and doing something unforgivable."

"You could just forgive us and let us go," Drakeforth suggested.

"It's too late. You have to be stopped."

I looked around. "We *have* been stopped. Goat! We're not moving!"

Goat snorted and woke from his reverie. "Goat?"

"We're run aground!" I yelled.

Goat ran to the rail and looked over. He dashed back to the odd collection of containers that stored his possessions and retrieved the rusty axe. With the weapon held high over his head, he ran to the various ropes that bisected the rail. Swinging wildly, he severed a goat hide rope and then looked over the rail.

With a growl, he took another swing. This one bounced off the harpoon cable and spun him in a circle. Goat steadied himself and smacked the rope with the axe again. This time the axe cut through the cable and buried itself deep in the wooden rail.

The airship bounced upwards and caught a prevailing wind, which sent us racing across the city at a fast walking pace.

Now freed from the restraining rope, Goat marched across the deck, murderous intent clear on his face.

"Easy, Goat," I intervened.

"Anchor...man," Goat snarled.

"Weird how he's sometimes in the here and now, and other times he's on an entirely different page," Eade said.

"Maybe you should go," Drakeforth said.

"Promise me you won't ruin everything," Eade insisted.

"I don't do promises," Drakeforth replied.

"He only ruins everything sometimes," I added.

Goat snatched up a coil of goat hide rope and pushed past me. He dropped a loop around Eade's waist, binding her arms to her sides.

"Hey, Goat, no!" I yelled. He brushed me aside and lifted Eade up. She yelled in terror and he casually tossed her over the rail. The goat-hide rope zipped out of its coil and we all rushed to grab it. Goat waited for a moment and then stamped a foot on the line. It went tight and creaked.

"Is she okay?" I asked.

"I guess so," Harenae said cautiously. "She didn't hit the ground, and there are some people untying her."

The line went slack and Goat reeled it back in. With an indignant sniff, he put the coiled rope back in its place amongst the rest of the detritus on deck.

I felt an awkward silence settle into place. Drakeforth walked off and started rummaging in the various shelves and boxes of debris that Goat had collected over time.

"What are you looking for?" I asked.

"That picture Goat had. The one of The Tree."

With little else to do, I helped him search.

We found the rolled-up skin in a battered metal trunk tied to one corner of the deck. Unrolling it on the table where Goat served tea, we stared at the crudely painted white shape on the smooth side of the skin.

"Well, there it is. Now what?" I asked.

"I had a thought," Drakeforth replied.

"You actually thought about something? Congratulations."

"Thank you. Remember how you said that The Tree was connected to everything?"

"I saw it... I think I saw it. The Tree is a conduit for empathic energy. An infinite number of streams endlessly cycling... Ohhh..."

"Exactly," Drakeforth replied. "The trick is finding it."

"Which we can't do because of the quantum properties of The Tree."

"You found it last time by not looking for it at all," Drakeforth said.

"It would help if we knew we were on the right track at least." I straightened up. "Harenae! Can you come here for a sec?"

"What's up?" she asked.

"Pathologists know the path, you said. What if the path isn't a road or a path at all? What if it is something else?

Harenae smiled. "You ever look at a map?" she asked. "I mean really *look* at it. Study a map long enough and you see beyond the lines. A map is a network, like the veins in your skin or the cracks in pyramid paving stones. Everything is connected. Pathologists can always follow the path until we arrive where we want to be."

"This drawing shows The Tree—you've heard of it, right?"

Harenae nodded and leaned over the rolled-out skin.

"This," Harenae said, pointing at the image of The Tree, "is out there."

"I hope so. Where, exactly?"

"Everywhere," Harenae replied. "The Tree is Living Oak. The paths are all around us."

"Empathic energy flows through the paths of The Tree…" I whispered.

"Could the Knotstick Order be using the interconnectedness of The Tree to transmit empathic energy to the pyramids?" I asked Drakeforth.

"Hardly seems like Godden Energy Corporation technology. They are more about the practical applications of double-e flux."

I felt a chill. "Which is why they need the Knotstick Order. Faith generates empathic energy, and The Tree allows them to move it across Pathia. How can that work?"

Drakeforth gave a rueful grimace. "Faith works in mysterious ways, Pudding. It happens because they believe it happens."

"Can we stop them" I asked.

"Stop people believing in something? Unlikely. We can illuminate, educate, and create doubt. That's enough work for anyone."

"Do something you love and you'll never work a day in your life, they say," I replied.

"Depends on what you love."

Something in his tone made me feel uncomfortable. I turned to the Pathologist. "Harenae, can you guide me? I want to follow the path to The Tree. I want to go everywhere, all at once."

"You sure?" she asked.

"Yeah, nah," I said.

"That means no," Harenae grinned.

"Nah, yeah?" I tried again.

"That just sounds weird. Follow me."

Harenae took my hand and placed it on the skin map. She took my other hand and turned towards the bow of the ship. I felt a chill ripple up my arm and, like an energy current, it pulsed through me and then exploded into perception.

CHAPTER 47

The pathologist walked ahead of me on a glittering path of light. Silicate grains winked and reflected internal fire. We left footprints that melted and ran like molten gold. Overhead, the stars spun in a time lapse of the Universe. Constellations formed as lines of double-e flux reached from point to point. Light pulsed along a neural network that touched us, moved through us, and left wire-frame structures in retina-burning after-glow.

The landscape formed and shadows took the form of cats, and the cats took the form of shadows. The Tree came together, as real and permanent as anything else I'd ever touched.

"We have arrived," Harenae announced.

"We never left," I smiled.

I walked around The Tree, seeing every mote of empathic energy flowing like sap from the roots up through the trunk and out to the furthest twigs and leaf tips. The energy flowed out into the dark sky, leaving trails of light in an endless cycle.

Empathic energy arced around my hand when I pressed it against the trunk. I disintegrated into light, particles and waves moving constantly until I reached the pyramids.

Why they had been built, I couldn't imagine. The vast spaces inside them were somewhere outside reality. Each a perfect pocket Universe overflowing with the raw energy of life.

The steady trickle of faith still flowed into the reservoirs. Soon the Godden Energy Corporation would arrive under the guise of some infrastructure project, and then pipes would be laid from the pyramid to the ports. The massive reserves of double-e flux would be pumped out of the desert and shipped overseas. Perhaps a campaign would be run to convince Pathians that empathic energy was the future. The refined particles of life would be sold back to the Pathians to power their televisions and toasters. Their faith in the knowledge they held dear would erode and be replaced by the digital credit system. Eventually the Credit Union would see the new economy they wanted, though I doubted they would recognise it when it came about.

A young man followed a herd of goats across the desert sand as the dunes and valleys moved under his feet like the ever-shifting waves of a restless ocean. He carried a small pot plant that he tended with what water he could make and the dirt from the goats.

His hair grew long and matted. The goats made more goats, and he made balloons from the guts of the ones he ate and used their hides as clothes. Scraps of wood and more goats were slowly built into a raft with a growing net of balloons that lifted him up and let him see further horizons.

The Tree bore persimmons, and he planted more trees. His drifting search took him from one side of the desert to the other, and then in a random zig-zagging pattern he followed the breeze. I saw things in a different light as he lived his nomadic life. Past, present, future, all blending and merging into a fractured mirror of his perceptions. The quest for the source of it all was his only anchor. No wonder he walked a different path.

A presence made itself felt and She was here as she had been since the moment I became aware in the double-e flux extraction tank at the Godden clinic.

"Hey," I said.

She smiled and ran her fingers through the curling streams. She knew each one, all these lives and all the others. She had been there for each of them in some way, in some guise, and always at the right moment.

I waited for her to speak, but she remained silent. I felt the pressure building, the remaining reservoirs of empathic energy taking on more than they ever had, now that the first pyramid had been destroyed.

Drakeforth sat on a park bench, a cat beside him, both pointedly ignoring each other. I stood next to him, staring along the well-lit path.

"I could release it all," I said.

"Yes," Drakeforth agreed.

"It wouldn't change anything. Not in the long run."

"It would make you feel better."

"I don't deserve to feel better."

Drakeforth stood up. "You have earned any reward you wish. You, Charlotte Pudding, have done more than anyone else has. You have sacrificed more than anyone could expect. For that, you will always have my gratitude and deepest respect."

"Drakeforth…"

"Death is the end, at least of this story."

"I'm dead?"

"Technically, dying. Of course you knew that. This is your final moment, your final breath. It lasts as long as you want it to. It ends when you give it away."

The woman with midnight hair and moon-glow skin took my hand in hers.

"She's never said a word," I whispered. "I don't even know her name."

"She never does, until you are ready to hear it. The people of the Aardvark Archipelago call her *Our Lady of the Last Breath*."

"Does she know what comes next?"

"You could ask her. I don't think it matters, though."

"Will you look after Goat? I think he may have found what he is looking for, and now he will need a new obsession."

Drakeforth sighed. "I'm not really the right person to be put in charge of someone else's wellbeing."

"You looked after me," I said.

"I was just trying to help while you had your hands full looking after me."

"Thanks, Vole."

"Oh, please, don't start getting all personal on me. People might think we were friends or something."

Drakeforth scratched the cat on the back of its head. It blinked at me and accepted his tribute.

"Goodbye, Pudding. I wish I could have been there to tell you to not be so damned selfless. She will take you from here. I have to accept that there is nothing more I can do."

"Goodbye, Drakeforth. Goodbye, Arthur. Think of me next time you have a cup of tea."

"I'll probably think of you next time I uncover a global conspiracy with horrific ethical and moral implications."

"I suggest you ignore it and have a cup of tea instead."

Drakeforth extended a hand, I shook it with the warmth of a close embrace, and then he was gone.

Feeling awkward, I asked, "So… What happens now?"

She smiled and leaned forward on tiptoes. Her lips brushed my ear and she whispered.